FATED FURY

FATE OF THE DARKMAGES
BOOK 1

ORLANDO A. SANCHEZ

BITTEN PEACHES
PUBLISHING

ABOUT THE STORY

Sometimes the safest place is in the midst of danger.

Darkmages die.

Everyone knew this.

Everyone accepted it...except her.

Meet Valentina, the last member of the Forza bloodline, a darkmage and granddaughter of Alfonse Forza—one of the most powerful and infamous Darkmages to walk the earth.

Until he disappeared without a trace.

The last known location of the Eclipse was inside the Mage Directorate Headquarters. She must now infiltrate the Directorate, locate the missing Eclipse, and somehow escape with her life.

Everything was going as planned, until her plan ran into Xander Ashford—Enforcer Xander Ashford, who has sworn to kill darkmages.

Now, Valentina must unleash her dormant darkmage powers, find and recover the Eclipse all while evading the Directorate and Inquisitor Emery, the lead mage who controls a relentless group of mage enforcers who follow only one law when it comes to darkmages.

Darkmages die.

"Never fear the darkness, for in it lies the power to create."
—Brandon Sanderson

"Don't be afraid of what lies in the darkness, because sometimes, the things hidden in the dark are our greatest allies."
—Israh Azizi

DEDICATION

*This one is for the Fathers,
who become so
by blood,
by choice,
by circumstance.*

*For Le Guin, Gaiman, and Pratchett.
Like wise and good teachers, you showed me the path, gave me a map,
and then challenged me to create my own way.*

Thank you.

AN INVITATION

An Invitation

An indie author writes with the hope and goal to share their worlds with their readers. I invite you to subscribe to my list for three FREE stories and my latest publishing news.

https://dl.bookfunnel.com/236fj6wv3f

ONE

New York City
Winter - 1925

Sid

A blast of frigid air cut through the streets.

I held onto her small hand, as she looked up at me through the fat flakes that had just begun falling. With a small smile I realized, that, like everything else in my life, timing was essential, and the context was decisive.

I looked down at my chronograph.

Any moment now.

We were several blocks away from our destination, but I knew we had been followed. The Directorate would have picked up on the same anomaly I was tracking when I first arrived on this plane.

They would send a triad to investigate, they would pick up on her signature, and I would be waiting to convince them it was a bad idea to apprehend and kill a child.

They would refuse to listen to reason, refuse to walk away. They would insist what the Directorate always insists.

Darkmages die.

It would be the worst and last day of their lives.

"Are they coming?" she asked in a small voice. "The bad men?"

I nodded, but refrained from turning around. There was no time for that, no time for fear.

No time at all.

"Yes, but I'm here now. We need to get you safe," I said, feeling anything but sure of myself. There were so many variables, tangents, and timelines. All of them jockeying for position, vying for preeminence.

This entire origin point in time was in flux.

"No time like the present," I said, sensing their energies coalesce around us. "Stay close."

The three mages materialized around us as we walked in the night. One in front and two behind—a typical triad formation.

They all wore the usual attire that distinguished the Mage Directorate from every other mage. Black combat armor, with their red sword in a crown insignia emblazoned over the left side of their chests.

Their black and red helms covered their faces, providing a method of keeping the mages' identities hidden.

In their hands, they held black and red neural batons, weapons designed to disrupt a mage's brain function by interrupting the central nervous system with a burst of energy, rendering the target mage ineffective and unable to form words, much less cast.

It was clear they were not anticipating much of a threat—these three were low-level mages, probably the lowest in the Directorate.

It was a mistake they would never repeat after tonight.

"No powers," I said under my breath as I gently squeezed her hand to get her attention. "Understand?"

"Yes," she said, examining the mage in front of us. There was no fear in her eyes, only a certain inevitability that the outcome had been decided. "You will stop them."

It wasn't a question, but a foregone conclusion.

I nodded and whispered a word of power unknown to the three mages around us. The subtle shift of power in the air around us went unnoticed, as expected.

"Give us the girl," the mage standing before us demanded. "Cooperate and you will be shown mercy."

"Really?" I said. "The mercy of a swift death?"

"More than a traitor like you deserves," said one of the mages behind us. "She's a darkmage and you're protecting her."

"Darkmages die," said the other mage behind us. "Everyone knows this...except you, it seems."

"Darkmages die," repeated the mage standing in front of us. The streets around us were strangely deserted as I glanced around. "I promise her death will be painless. I can't say the same for you."

"How merciful of you," I said, glancing down at the young girl next to me. "I'm sorry to inform you that she's not mine to give to you, and I will have to refuse your request tonight. However, I do have a counter offer."

"A counter—?" the lead mage sputtered, clearly not accustomed to rebellion. "Do you know who you are speaking to?"

"The Mage Directorate," I said. "From the looks of you three—a triad tasked with bringing in low-level renegade mages—you never expected to encounter a darkmage tonight, am I right?"

From the silence and the look of uncertainty on the lead's face, I knew I was right. I almost pitied them, until I remembered that they were prepared to erase and kill the young child holding my hand.

My pity quickly transformed into a seething, barely controlled fury.

"Comply or we will end you where you stand," the lead mage said. "There is no escape. Do the right thing."

"End?" I said, keeping my rage in check. "You will *end* me? How sanitized. Why don't you call it what it is...murder. An unjustified, unprovoked killing."

"We're following our orders," he said. "You are in violation of statute one, section one. Fail to comply and we will respond with deadly force."

"Do *you* know who you're talking to?" I asked. "Do you know who I am?"

"I know all I need to know," the lead mage replied. "A traitor who would stand against the Directorate to defend a darkmage. You're scum, lower than scum, for protecting that abomination."

"I've been called worse," I said as they activated their batons. I glanced at her again. "Stay next to me."

TWO

With another whispered word of power, I shattered time around us, bringing it to a stop. With a gesture, I formed three silver orbs, while the mages around us froze in place.

"You froze them?" she asked. "I thought you said no powers?"

"For *you*," I said, focused on the orbs hovering in the air before me. "I'll be gone before they assemble a group of mages strong enough to deal with what they're picking up right now."

"What did you do?" she asked. "They're not frozen with ice, but they can't move."

"I don't freeze the way you do, little fox," I said. "They are frozen in time. Right now, if we were counting, they would be stuck between the one and the two."

"Oh," she said, looking intently at the mages around us, but remaining close to me. "Will you unfreeze them?"

"Yes, but not now," I said. "Those orbs will send them to a different when."

"A different when?"

"A moment in time earlier than this one," I explained. "I

will send them back in time about an hour. I don't dare do more—that would attract too much attention."

"You won't kill them?" she asked, her voice hard and her eyes steel. "You will let them live? Why?"

I crouched down in front of her.

"If you remember anything from tonight, I want you to remember this," I said, taking both her hands in mine and staring into her eyes. "Just because you can wield your power, doesn't mean you should. Do you understand?"

She nodded and glanced at the three mages again.

"They wanted to kill me."

"Yes," I said. "If you kill them now, you become no better than these mindless pawns following the twisted dictates of an antiquated order, and you...you are so much better."

Let me get my hands bloody now. Yours should remain clean for as long as possible; once you begin, the bloodshed will be staggering.

She nodded.

I truly hoped she understood.

I released the orbs and they gently collided with the three mages simultaneously. In moments, they vanished from sight.

"That's going to get some real attention," I continued. "We need to go...now."

We ran for several blocks until I was sure we had arrived at the safe house that would be her home.

"Here?" she asked when I drew us up short in front of the newly constructed townhouse. "Is this it?"

"This will be your new home," I said, touching several of the symbols on the walls of the townhouse. The runes on the door flared to life with orange energy as the door opened. "Inside, quickly."

We stepped into the townhouse. I closed the door behind us and activated the nullification runes. For all intents and purposes, we were now invisible to all mages seeking our signatures.

"How long do we have to stay here?" she asked. "Are they coming?"

"You're safe now," I said. "You will stay here for some time. I will not be staying long."

"You're leaving me here alone?"

"Alone? Never," I said. "I will leave you in the very secure hands of your Guardians. One of them will be here shortly."

I glanced down at my chronometer.

He would be arriving in two minutes.

The second Guardian would take some coaxing, and if I botched the introduction, he could very easily shred us to small parts in a fit of anger.

No pressure.

"Why don't you take off your coat and wait in the main room," I suggested. "He will be here soon."

She shrugged off her coat and hung it on one of the hooks provided in the space just off the entrance. She made her way to the adjoining room while I waited for the first of my guests.

THREE

Fen

I walked the frigid streets of New York in the dead of night.

My old bones protested at the cold, and I cursed myself for accepting the invitation. I looked at the address I was given—41 Commerce Street—and matched it to the building I currently stood in front of.

The property was heavily runed and I wondered what game the Traveler was playing.

I knocked several times.

The runes on the door bloomed to life and then dimmed. The door opened and remained ajar several moments later.

I looked in tentatively.

"Hello?" I called out. "Anyone home?"

"In here," a familiar voice called out. "Come in!"

I entered the home, thankful for the warmth. The foyer led to a short hallway which led to a large sitting room where I saw the Traveler and a young girl.

She was seated behind a large table on the other side of

the room, next to the Traveler, who held a large mug of steaming liquid.

One sniff told me it was coffee.

Dark, rich, delicious coffee.

I gazed into her deep, penetrating gaze. Her hazel eyes shone with a latent power, and I cursed.

Nothing good could come of this.

If I were smart, I would turn around this very moment and walk out the door.

But I couldn't.

I owed him.

With a sigh of resignation, I took off my coat and hung it up before venturing farther into the sitting room. I looked across at the Traveler and scowled. He smiled back, before taking another sip from his steaming mug.

He pointed to a mug on the table, indicating it was for me. I took hold of it and drank, warming my body, and savoring the potent taste.

The coffee was excellent.

I took a seat at the table and gazed at the Traveler and the girl. Whatever this was, I had a feeling deep in my bones that it was dangerous and potentially lethal.

"You're looking good, Fen," he said. "How long has it been?"

I remained silent for a few moments, as I stared at him.

"Three decades, give or take," I said. "You look the same."

"I have a tendency to do that," he said, dismissing my words with a wave. "Thank you for accepting my invitation."

"I don't mean to sound rude," I said warily. "Why am I here?"

He leaned back in his chair and stared at me. His usual black peacoat hung off the back of his chair, and he wore a white dress shirt, blue jeans, and brown boots. He ran a hand through his unruly hair and smiled again.

"Her," he said, cocking his head in the little girl's direction. "She is the reason you're here."

"Say again?" I asked, looking at the little girl closer now. "What are you saying?"

The little girl looked down at her hands, avoiding eye contact with me. She wore a thick dress with edges of fur, boots, and a defiant look. Her black hair was pulled back into a tight ponytail and her pale skin shone with a subtle inner light. My instinct informed me this child was dangerous.

My instinct was never wrong.

She snuck a few glances at me. I could tell from her looks that she didn't fear me, which was a surprise.

I usually scared everyone.

"She needs your help."

"Are you actively trying to get me killed?" I asked. "That is not a rhetorical question."

"How many times has that been attempted?" he asked, the smile never leaving his face. "I mean I tried at *least* five times. Given your circle of enemies, I'm certain it's more than that."

"I stopped keeping count after twenty."

"Yet here you sit," he said, motioning to me with his mug. "Is there a way to do it?"

"A way to do what?"

"Kill you?"

I gave him a glare.

"I'm not immortal," I said. "Of course there's a way."

"Care to share?"

"I said I'm not immortal, I didn't say I was an idiot," I growled back. "Why in the name of everything unholy am I in this godforsaken country enduring this cold?"

"As I said earlier, she needs your help."

I gave the young girl another long look.

"No," I said, my voice firm, shaking my head. "I'm not a babysitter and I don't like children, *any* children."

"Nevertheless, she needs your help," he said. "*You* are the perfect choice."

"Didn't you hear what I just said?" I asked, glancing at her again. "No. Where are her parents?"

"Indisposed...permanently."

I scowled. I knew what that meant.

The child was an orphan.

"Then the answer is hell no," I said, getting to my feet. "No offense, child. Sid, thank you for the coffee and having me come here in the winter to freeze my as—my nether regions off," I amended with a glance at the child."

"You're welcome."

"Whatever this is," I said as I waved an arm at the two of them, "I don't want any of it."

Black energy formed around the girl, shimmering in the air around her body, as strands of her black hair transformed to a bright white.

I extended my left hand and forced my will into my arm, materializing my blade—Darkdrinker.

"I would advise against that course of action, my friend," he said. "Please, sit."

"Bleed me dry, she's a darkmage?" I said, sitting and staring at the girl now. "Darkmages die. You know this. I know this. Everyone knows this. The Mage Directorate will crucify me if I let her live. That is not a metaphor."

"I thought they tried crucifixion already?"

"It didn't take," I said, eyeing the child warily. "What is it?"

"*She* is a child that needs your help," he said. "Every timeline where she is alone, she ends up dying. I need her alive. This world needs her alive. The only way to facilitate that is to get her a Guardian, so I got her two. You are one of them."

"Is she really a child?"

"Well," he said, glancing at her, "she ages very slowly as most mages do, but I can assure you, she is very much a child at this present moment."

"How old is she, exactly?" I asked, glancing at the child and keeping my distance. "Real years."

"What year are we currently in?"

"You don't know what year it is?"

"On this plane?" he said, shaking his hand. "It all gets a little wibbly-wobbly, timey-wimey."

"Very scientific description there," I said, shaking my head. "It's currently 1925 on *this* plane."

"Hmm," he said, rubbing his chin and glancing at the child. "She has been kept secure by some of my associates since she was born."

"Kept secure? Why would she need to be kept secure?"

"We'll get to that in a minute," he said, raising a finger. "That was at the turn of the century, so around twenty five years ago, but since she's a mage her aging is considerably delayed."

"She's twenty-five years old?" I asked, mildly shocked. "She doesn't look a day over five."

"Mages age slowly," he said. "I *did* mention this, yes?"

"I'm aware, I just didn't think it would be that slow."

"The ratio of apparent age to true age is a direct reflection of the power of the mage in question," he said. "The stronger the mage the slower they age."

"You just said she was twenty-five."

"Yes, she is currently twenty-five, but appears to be five," he said. "She ages one year for every five chronological years that pass. I expect that ratio will only increase as she matures and grows in power."

I glanced at the child again.

Her eyes were vibrant with a deep intelligence. From her

furtive looks, I could tell she understood everything we had been discussing.

"Why are you doing this to me?" I protested. "I thought we were friends? You know my life, what I do. She'll be dead within a week hanging around me. Not hurt—dead. I have enough difficulties with the Directorate's Hounds after me."

"Sometimes the safest place is right in the midst of danger."

"Rubbish," I said. "Being near me is no place for a child, darkmage or not. You said her parents were de—gone? Is she being hunted?"

"She has a particular set of traits," he said, measuring his words. "Traits that the Directorate consider dangerous—tainted."

"She's a darkmage," I said. "I'm going to have to agree on the *tainted* idea. Frankly, I'm surprised she's still breathing."

"Not for lack of trying," he said. "The Directorate attempted to retire her earlier today."

"That is exactly what I mean," I said. "They *will* come for her."

"I know. It's your job to make sure she remains breathing," he said, staring at me. "I need you to keep her alive and safe."

I shook my head slowly.

"There has to be someone else, someone insane—well, more insane than me—who could do this."

"There's only one Fenrir the Feared," he said, calling up memories long since forgotten. "You're the most accomplished Guardian of the Directorate."

"No one calls me that anymore," I said. "It's just Fen these days."

"Still, you have the most impressive reputation amongst the Guardians of the Directorate."

"Had. I'm an ex-Guardian," I corrected. "They did try to kill me. Remember?"

"Details."

"It's where the devil dwells."

"Irrelevant," he said, waving my words away. "*You* are the most qualified for this task."

"Who else did you ask?" I asked. "Tell me you asked someone else. Anyone?"

"Not a soul," he said. "This child's presence needs to be kept secret until she's ready."

"Ready? Ready for what?"

"Ready for what only she can do," he said. "She has a specific task to accomplish."

"Why does this task sound fatal for those around her?"

"Right now, the world is a big place," he said. "There will be a time when it will become a significantly smaller place. She needs to be ready by then. I need you to keep her alive and safe until that time comes."

"Does she have a name?" I asked, looking at the little girl again. "What do you call her?"

"Her name is Valentina Forza," he said, and my blood ran cold. "I call her Val or Kitsune. You may want to ask her what she prefers."

FOUR

Fen

"Forza?" I asked, barely able to form the words. "As in Darkmage Alfonse Forza?"

He nodded.

"House Forza was hunted into obscurity and frankly, few know if any survived the Directorate purge," he said. "She may be Alfonse's only living relative."

"You're saying she's a blood relative of the bane of the Directorate?" I asked in disbelief. "*That* Forza?"

"The one and the same," he said with a slight smile. "You can see why the Directorate would be eager to apprehend his *grandchild*."

"Apprehend?" I said. "How are we not currently surrounded at the moment by a Directorate Task Force attempting to break down the door, to end her life and eliminate us for being here?"

"They don't know where she is—yet," he said with a pause. "They are aware, however, that she exists."

"And what happened earlier this evening?"

"I took care of it," he said. "That Triad won't remember ever meeting her."

"Alfonse has been missing for years," I said, "right after he executed a squadron of Mage Directorate Hounds who made the mistake of trying to apprehend him."

"Last mistake they made," he said. "How many did they lose that day?"

"Fifty of some of their best trained mages," I said, remembering the day Alfonse Forza declared war on the Mage Directorate. "All of them against one darkmage...and they lost."

"Spectacularly. He's not just any darkmage," Sid said. "Forza was exceptional, even among darkmages. Only Quinn could match him in skill and ferocity."

"What happens if they discover who she is?"

"What better way to bring him out of hiding?" he said. "Rumor has it that he is quite fond of this child, considering she inherited his abilities."

"Do you know how to find him?"

"I have my sources," he said. "I *may* know where he is."

"Then contact him and give *her* to him," I said. "Sounds like the best solution."

"Out of the question," he said, shaking his head. "He would only weaponize her. Or kill her outright. That is unacceptable."

"She's his family."

"She poses a considerable threat to him," he said. "I need her safe until she grows into her power. Her family won't do, so I found the next best thing."

"Me?"

"You."

"You must be delusional. I'm not a darkmage and don't use energy that way," I said. "Find a darkmage. Did you try finding a darkmage?"

"None would qualify," he said. "I need someone with your particular set of skills and characteristics."

I narrowed my eyes at him.

"They all said no, didn't they?"

"They all said no," he answered with a slight smile. "Something about it being suicide."

"Which it is," I said. "Forza killed Directorate Hounds as a hobby. He once blasted an entire compound of Directorate mages because he was in a bad mood. He is the reason darkmages have the reputation they have. He is what is called...a Bad Person."

"I'm aware."

I glanced at Valentina again.

"And you have his grandchild because you've grown tired of living?"

"I have her because she is crucial to an event I'm not at liberty to share—at least not yet."

"Thanks for being so clear. Why am *I* here, then?"

"I thought I explained this?"

"Explain it again."

"You are here to make sure she stays alive."

"Does she possess the power of speech?" I asked. "Or is she mute? She's surprisingly quiet for a child."

He gave me a withering look.

"Yes," he said, "she can speak and has understood every word we have uttered, despite her outward appearance of youth."

"Do you know how to control her power?"

"She hasn't entered into her power...not yet."

"Not yet?" I asked, surprised. "She is a darkmage. They're not known for gentle or friendly abilities. It's usually all death and destruction with them."

"Well then, it's a good thing she has you as her Guardian, isn't it?"

"No, nothing about this is good," I said. "The Directorate will be after us once they realize she is dark."

"They already have that information," he said. "Your job—your *only* job—is to make sure they don't find her or worse."

"What are you going to do in the meantime?"

"I'm going to make sure that when the student is ready, the teacher appears," he said. "In the meantime"—he reached into a pocket of his coat—"until she is ready, it would be a good idea to make sure she always wears this."

He placed a simple black ring on the table.

It was covered in black energy and emanated power. It was enough power to give me pause.

"That artifact," I said, pointing at the ring and shoving my chair back. "That thing...that ring is cursed."

He ran a golden chain through the ring and slid it across the table to me. It stopped short of my mug and pulsed with power, mocking me.

"Deadly, not cursed," he said, pointing at the ring. "That ring belonged to her father and her grandfather before him. Now it's hers."

"What makes you think I want to hold it?"

"It's not for *you*," he repeated. "It's a failsafe for her, until her powers manifest. It will give her a degree of control until she can control her powers on her own."

"If it's meant for her, how did you get it?" I asked.

"Her father gave it to her before...well, before they were apprehended by the Directorate," he said, pointing at the ring. "You'll need to keep it safe as well. I hear it's quite infamous in the wrong circles."

"That thing is also supposed to lead to the Eclipse—Forza's blade which was shattered," I said. "It's supposed to allow for the locating and rejoining of the blade."

"Rumor and conjecture, from what I hear," he said before

taking another sip of his coffee. "Forza will want it back. You cannot let him get his hands on her or that ring."

"You *are* trying to get me killed."

"Not in the least."

"Forget the child for a moment," I said, my voice grim. "The Eclipse is known to every Guardian in the Directorate. This ring is practically screaming to be discovered. How am I supposed to hide it without dying in the process?"

"The chain," he said, pointing at the golden chain attached to the ring. "Obfuscation runes. No one will know what you are carrying as long as you don't remove the ring from the chain."

"You want me to protect a darkmage child and hide the key to one of the most infamous blades known to Guardians, *and* stay alive?"

"See? I knew you would understand the mission," he said, getting to his feet and brushing off his pants. "I'm afraid you'll have to remain here for a few decades."

"A few decades?" I asked. "How many decades exactly?"

"Seven to ten," he said. "At least until her powers manifest fully."

"You want me to watch her for a century?"

"Or until her powers manifest fully," he clarified. "It could be earlier."

"Or it could be a century."

"It's safe for now, but that will change. You have everything you need on the property. Once the city grows, you'll have to move. I'll meet with you then."

"A century?" I said. "I'm supposed to remain in this backwater city for a century?"

"It won't always be a backwater, trust me," he said. "Eventually, this city will be one of the most important cities in the plane. Until then, the runes around the property will keep you hidden from Forza. As for everyone else—this place is virtually invisible."

"Virtually," I said with a grumble. "That doesn't mean completely."

"I also added some aversion runes which will keep the Directorate Hounds away from this region for some time," he continued. "They won't be able to bypass those runes for at least a century or more."

"I see," I said. "Don't I have a say in this?"

"There's a very well-stocked library, and her abilities won't manifest until she hits puberty, at least," he continued, ignoring me. "Let her read and explore the house, but keep her in your sight at all times."

"This is not right; a child like her should be in a proper home with her family, her parents, going to school, and living a regular life."

"That is not the hand she was dealt, Fen," he said, his voice grim. "Much like you don't get a 'say' in this situation, this child will *never* live a regular life. As for her family, *you* are now her family, her *only* family."

"Don't forget her deranged grandfather."

"We're not including homicidal darkmages in that equation," he said. "You are now her *only* family."

"Earlier, you mentioned another Guardian?"

"Not yet," he said. "She is still too young. How do you feel about honey badgers?"

The question threw me.

"Honey badgers?" I asked. "What? To eat? I've never hunted one. Are they tasty? Is the meat sweet?"

He gave me a look and shook his head.

"I worry about you sometimes, Fen," he said. "You really need to get out more. I strongly advise against trying to hunt this particular honey badger."

"You have one here?" I asked concerned, looking around. "It's in the house? What does it look like?"

"They look like raccoons, but are vicious and deadly," he said. "Nevermind, he'll show up when she's ready. I just don't know where. It's not locked down. This would be so much easier if I could pinpoint the variables."

I looked at him.

"You worry about *me* sometimes?" I said. "I worry about your brain every time we meet. What are you going on about?"

He waved my words away.

"Never mind. His name is Melvichor Ratel, Mel for short. He is her second, more ferocious Guardian. Not that you aren't ferocious in your own right. I think you two will get along great. Oh, I forgot to mention, he's a changeling. It's almost like you're cousins."

"Shifters and changelings are not related."

"Don't shifters and changelings share the same common ancestry?"

"No," I said. "We are nothing alike. Not even close."

"Oh, I thought you were related somehow," he said. "In any case, you two are tasked with keeping her safe and alive. Do try to get along."

"A changeling?" I asked. "You want me to protect a changeling as well as a child?"

"If you had ever encountered a honey badger, you wouldn't ask that question."

"Honey badgers are supposed to be dangerous?" I asked. "You just said he's like a raccoon. The only times raccoons are dangerous is when they're rabid."

"You omitted the ferocious, vicious, and deadly part of the description," he said. "He won't need protecting; his job is to bond with and protect her. Think of Mel as your assistant Guardian, able to easily infiltrate places you can't—like the

Directorate. Hmm"—he tapped his chin—"it's possible he'll show up there. These bifurcating timelines make a mess out of everything."

"I'm not seeing this honey badger as a major threat," I said. "You couldn't find another shifter? I'd feel more comfortable with another shifter."

"Surprisingly, the combination of her lineage, and your reputation didn't seem to encourage many applicants for the position of assistant Guardian."

"Imagine that," I said, glancing at the child. "People were reluctant to take on a suicide Guardianship. Color me surprised."

"I know, right?" he said. "Me too."

"I'm not a mage, much less a darkmage. You want me to train her?"

"A source that I can trust informed me that you were an excellent tutor to several of the Guardian trainees in multiple disciplines, such as swordplay and warfare. Even mages need to learn how to fight, not everything is spells and casting."

"I was a tutor under protest."

"Be that as it may, use the time to teach her everything you know," he said, heading for the door. "Enhance your skills as well. You could stand to polish your abilities. There's no better way to do that, besides teaching another. She needs to get stronger."

"You want her to get *stronger*?"

"She *must* get stronger," he said. "Your part in her life is essential, Fen. The time will come when she will have to leave you."

"If she doesn't kill me first."

"Always a possibility."

"Not very reassuring."

"You must keep her alive and safe until her powers manifest."

"What happens when they do?"

"Her time with you will draw to a close," he answered. "When her powers manifest she will need instruction. Since you are not a darkmage, you will send her here." He handed me a card with some writing on it. "Give her that; Moira will know what to do."

"And until then?" I asked. "What am I to do with her?"

"Get her ready."

"Ready for what?"

"She's a Forza, what do you think? Get her ready for war."

"War? Against whom?"

"The Pentarch will want her ability, the Directorate will want her under control, the darkmages will want her martyrdom, and her grandfather will want her unswerving loyalty or death. I'd say against everyone."

"Any chance the Directorate or Forza will let this go?"

"Not while she's breathing," he said. "She and that sword pose a major threat to the Directorate, one they need to eliminate."

"And Forza?"

"Will attempt to use her as a weapon to eliminate his enemies," he said, his expression dark. "We can't let that happen."

"Decades," I said, shaking my head. "And then where? The Directorate is everywhere."

"Slowly, this city will transform," he said. "In time, you will have allies. I have safe houses everywhere, trust me."

"Trusting you is how I ended up in this situation in the first place," I said, pointing at him. "You owe me, huge."

"I know," he said. "Don't worry, I always pay my debts."

The next moment, he stepped out into the cold.

The door closed quietly behind him, leaving me alone with a darkmage child and a cursed ring.

FIVE

New York City
Present day

Valentina

Before every training session he would do this, not that I minded. If I hurried, I would get outside just in time for the Enforcer Patrol shift change.

I rushed outside and made it to the local deli on the corner of Barrow and Bleecker streets just as they turned the corner. I checked my watch—three-thirty A.M. I had half an hour before Fen read me the riot act.

I ducked into the deli, picked up the gallon of milk, and stealthily kept my eye on the two Enforcers that had begun their patrol. It was the only part of my four A.M. training that I looked forward to.

It was always the same two Enforcers. One was tall, slim, alert and handsome in a rugged way. He was always scanning the perimeter and had almost caught me looking at them a few times.

The other was short and stocky. He too, kept an eye on their surroundings, but his expression was a mix of anger and disgust. He gave off major dangerous vibes, and I made it a point to give him plenty of space.

Last thing I needed was the attention of Directorate Enforcers. Though I wouldn't mind getting the attention of tall, slim, and handsome.

That would be perfect, right up to the moment he discovers you are a darkmage. Then he'd have to kill you.

Darkmages die.

That would definitely put a damper on our first date. Still, it didn't hurt to imagine his strong arms around my—

"Hello?" Patricia, the deli owner, said after clearing her voice with a cough. "Are you paying for that, or are you going to spend all morning staring at the Enforcers?"

"Was I that obvious?"

"Only every morning you manage to get here at three-thirty sharp to catch a glimpse of the tall, handsome one. I don't blame you, he is a fine specimen, mmhmm."

"Yes, he is," I said. "And he doesn't even know I exist."

"Better that way," Patricia said, shaking her head. "Directorate Enforcers are dangerous, and most, if not all of them, are only focused on Directorate business. Stay away from them."

I nodded, paid for the milk and ran home.

I made it back and inside by three-fifty, with ten minutes to spare. I still had to be on the training floor by four A.M. sharp, or Fen would 'encourage' me to be on time with extra drills and pushups.

They were never very encouraging.

I made it upstairs—the training floor was on the top level—with two minutes to spare. I caught my breath and composed myself as I stepped onto the actual training floor.

A glowering Fen waited for me with crossed arms and a scowl.

"I sensed you a block away," he said. "You let yourself get distracted, again."

"I masked," I said. "No one saw or sensed me, no one besides you and Patricia."

He towered over me, at least a foot taller and several hundred pounds heavier.

"You have to be able to mask better, Kit," he said, his voice low and gruff. "The way I taught you. They'll kill you if they find out the truth."

"I know," I said, focusing on my mask. "Darkmages die."

He nodded, his expression serious.

"We can't control where or when we are born," he said, "but we can control what we do with the power we have."

He held a short, rune-covered staff in his hand. It was about four feet in length and equal to the one I held. I stifled a yawn, knowing that would earn me pushups and drills until my arms fell off.

This training had to qualify as torture somewhere.

It was still the middle of the night, or early morning as Fen liked to call it—it didn't matter at what time we trained, it was early morning...somewhere.

Today it was a four A.M. training.

There were nights he would surprise me awake, just to keep me *ready*, as he called it. No matter the time, he always seemed as fresh as if it were the middle of the afternoon. I clamped down on another yawn. I just wanted to go back to bed and sleep for a few more hours, if not days.

"Darkmages die," I said, serious. "I hate that saying. I hate the fact that it's true even more."

"Why is your training so harsh, Kit?" Fen asked, his voice softening slightly when it looked like I wanted to quit, which was every time we started training. "Tell me."

"Because my enemies will show me no mercy," I said. "They will hunt me and those I care for relentlessly, until I'm dead or I end them. I hate them."

"No," he said, glancing off to the side for a brief second. "You must not let hate take root in your heart. Tell me why."

I recalled the lesson.

He had been teaching me this lesson for as long as I knew him, which was most of my life.

"Hate festers and grows."

"What else?"

"It makes one easy to control and manipulate, robbing clarity of thought," I said, remembering the answers. "Hate destroys reason."

"And?"

"When you operate from hate, you end up dead, sooner rather than later," I said. "Hate makes you easy to exploit and eliminate. Hate will get me killed."

He nodded and swung his staff a few times.

"No matter how much you want to, and I understand the desire, you must not let hate control you," he said and paused. "The power you will wield, the power within you, if you give in to hate, will take control. You will become consumed by it."

"Like my grandfather?"

"Like your grandfather," he said, his voice somber. "That's why I'm hard on you, Kit, harder than I've been with any of my students. I need to make sure that the day you face him—"

"He's been missing forever."

"Missing doesn't mean dead," he said. "When you face him, I need to make sure he won't turn you, that you will be strong enough to stand against him, physically and mentally. I will not have you filled with hate."

"It's hate and ignorance that kills Darkmages."

"Only if they allow themselves to be killed." He stood there, glaring at me. "You intend on being a statistic? Did I raise and train you to become a statistic?"

"No."

"Then focus harder."

"I *am* focusing harder."

"You know how many darkmages the Directorate killed last year?" he asked. "How many were exterminated just for being darkmages? For existing?"

"Doesn't matter," I said, gritting my teeth as I worked on focusing. "Even one, is one too many."

He nodded again.

"Exactly," he said. "I can still sense your ability. Which means—"

"I'm dead," I said, letting out a long breath and collapsing to the floor. "This is impossible."

"Really?" he said, approaching me. "Sense me, Kitsune, and don't half ass it."

He was the only one in my life allowed to call me that—Kitsune were trickster fox creatures with supernatural abilities. Fen abbreviated the nickname to Kit when he was trying to get me to focus on some lesson.

Or he was in a cranky mood, which was usually when he was awake.

"Today, Kit," he said with a low growl. "I'm not getting any younger."

I nodded, stood, and focused my darksight. Every mage had some version of darksight. The Directorate called it an innersight. Darkmages called it the darksight. They were similar but not identical.

Innersight was rational, operating on energy signatures and the presence of power.

Darksight operated from emotions. Sensing strong emotions came easily to me—it also meant my strong emotions could betray me. Darksight could also sense signatures, but emotions were the easiest for me.

I opened my darksight and got...nothing.

Fen was standing right in front me, closer to looming and scowling, and he may as well have been invisible. Nothing came across—he was a void, an empty space in front of me.

"What do you sense?" he asked. "Tell me."

"More like, what don't I sense."

"Clarify."

"I get nothing," I said, giving up after a few more seconds of searching. "You're not even there. I sense nothing."

"No, incorrect," he said his voice steel. "Try again, and this time focus harder."

I glared at him, but he stood his ground.

I took a deep breath and focused, trying again. It wasn't that he was invisible—my darksight had nothing to grab onto or sense. He was non-existent.

"You don't...I don't know how to explain it—it's like you're a hole in space. There's a Fen-sized hole in front of me, and I can't get my darksight to locate you no matter how hard I try. How do you mask like that?"

"It's not masking," he said. "Masking is easy. You blend your signature to the energy around you and you disappear."

"Why can't I learn that?"

"Because the Mage Directorates—the real skilled ones—will see right through a mask," he said. "They'll find your weak attempt at blending and tear you apart before you realize you're being attacked. That's why you can't learn *that*."

"Okay, that sounds like a bad idea."

"The worst," he said with a nod. "What I'm teaching you is beyond masking. You're learning to deepcloak. Think of it as an advanced mask—the most advanced mask, in fact. Which you will need because...?"

"Because we can't attack the Directorate from the

outside," I said around a yawn that managed to escape me. He gave me a sharp look as I cut it short. "Sorry."

"Not as sorry as you will be. Down, don't touch," he snapped, pointing to the floor. "We'll start with one hundred and see if you wake up by the time they're done."

I groaned as I dropped to the floor.

"Did I hear a groan of excited anticipation? Fantastic. I always enjoy when you share your enthusiasm with me. Make it two hundred. Are we excited enough to go for three?"

"No, sir," I said entering push up position. "Not sharing at all."

"Pity," he said, tapping his staff on the floor. "Begin."

I began my torture of pushups.

"Tell me why we can't attack the Directorate from the outside?" he said as he walked over to the kitchen area and poured himself some coffee. "Why?"

I didn't dare pause my pushups. He had uncanny hearing and would know if I paused to catch my breath and add another hundred just for the attempt.

"The information we need is only located inside the Directorate," I said in-between pushups. "I need to infiltrate them and become a Directorate Agent."

"Where inside?"

"All the information on my grandfather and the Eclipse is kept secure inside the Directorate HQ," I said as my arms burned. "The only way to get that information is to get inside and access the restricted archives and artifact vaults."

"Correct," he said, taking a long sip from his mug as he watched me. "This is some excellent coffee." He held up the mug and admired it. "Thank you. You have outdone yourself today, Kit."

"My pleasure," I managed through short breaths. My arms and chest were on fire. "I still think this is doing things the hard way."

"Oh, you're *thinking* now?" Fen said, tapping his staff on the floor near my head. "Will wonders never cease? We do this my way, until you come up with a better plan."

"A better plan would be letting me get at least six hours of sleep," I muttered under my breath. "*That* would be a better plan."

"Excuse me?" he said, crouching down near my head. "You have something you want to share? Please, illuminate me."

"Just that these insane middle of the night training sessions would be easier if we did them when I was awake."

"On your feet," he said, his voice steel as I stood immediately. "Deepcloak now."

He wasn't asking. Either I deepcloaked or I would be introduced to his staff—repeatedly.

I hated that staff.

I focused and aligned myself to the energy around me reflexively. I deepcloaked my energy signature until I was 'invisible' to any kind of magical scanning. It felt like holding my breath under water while my lungs wanted to explode.

"Fear is an excellent motivator," he said, pointing at me with his staff. "That is a decent deepcloak. It could still use some polish, but it's acceptable. Good work."

I nodded, maintaining my focus.

He stepped into a fighting stance, loosely holding his staff. He stared into my eyes and let out a long breath, his yellow eyes boring into mine. I circled around, stepping into my own fighting stance.

"When will you be attacked?" he asked. "When will it happen?"

"When I least expect it."

"How will you react?"

"Instinctively, without thought," I said. "My response will be reflex, automatic."

"How will that happen?"

"Practice, unending practice, followed by more practice."

"When will you surrender?" he asked. "At what point do you submit?"

"When I exhale my last breath."

"What do Darkmages do?"

"Darkmages overcome and conquer."

"Good."

Then he attacked.

Fen was enormous, but he moved like someone half his size. His staff thrust forward, aimed at my head.

It was nearly too fast to track.

I ducked, sliding under his attack, and lunged forward with an attack of my own. He side-stepped my thrust, parrying my staff with his own, as he rotated his weapon and brought it down to crush my skull.

I raised my staff and angled it away, deflecting his blow and letting it slide to the floor next to me. In the same motion, I turned and brought my staff down to smash into his face.

He rotated around my attack, leading with a spinning backfist designed to remove my head from my shoulders.

If I let it connect.

I ducked under the fist, knowing there was no way I could block or parry that attack. The displacement of air rushed past me, as his tree trunk of an arm whooshed above my head.

He outclassed me on sheer mass and power.

I would have to use that against him.

While crouched, I slammed my staff into his knee. The goal was to shatter his knee and follow up with a blow to his head. He sensed the plan even before I executed the strike.

He turned his leg, catching my staff behind his knee, while drawing a blade from his thigh sheath.

He slashed at my hand, and I let go of the staff to keep my

fingers attached. I rolled to the side, creating distance between us as he took hold of my staff with his opposite hand.

"No primary weapon," he said, keeping his voice low and dropping his staff. "Now what?"

"My greatest weapon rests between my ears," I said, reaching down to my thigh and unsheathing my blade. "I still have that one."

"Having it and using it are two different things," he said, tossing my staff away as he entered a blade stance with a smile. "You ready to surrender?"

"Not in this lifetime," I said, circling around again. "That knee catch was a dirty move."

"No such thing, and you know it," he said. "What are the rules?"

"There are no rules," I said, watching his blade warily. My concern kicked up a few notches. Fen could use almost any weapon, but he preferred blades, which meant we worked them the most. "You never said we were working blades today."

"I wasn't aware I needed to inform you of every weapon we were going to train with," he said with a shrug. "A little surprise here and there keeps you on your toes."

"Just would've appreciated the heads-up."

"Expect the unexpected," he said. "Every darkmage operates with this tenet in mind. You certainly better learn to do so."

"Expect the unexpected? Really? That's your answer?"

"There's been a change of plans," he said. "A fight, duel, or battle are fluid things, constantly in flux. One moment, it's a staff you're facing, and the next it's a blade. Adapt or die."

"This is really going to hurt," I muttered under my breath.

I weighed my options as I looked for openings.

They were grim.

I had a choice between bad and worse.

Fen being a blademaster meant that if I practiced in actual combat for the next half century, I would only be scratching the surface of his skill.

That was the bad choice.

The worse option was that his blades were nullblades—runed against magic. Even if I managed to find or create an opening, there was little I could do with it.

His skill dwarfed mine.

I had lost this fight even before the first attack.

"What is the best way to engage in a knife duel and escape unscathed?" he continued. "How is it done?"

"Not engage in the duel at all?"

He nodded.

"A good option if you can pull it off," he said, switching blade hands. "Suffice to say, that option is no longer available to you. What is the next best method to escape unscathed?"

"Overwhelming force."

"Can you manage it and not give yourself away?"

"Do I have a choice?"

"None that I'm giving you," he said. "Better act before it's too late."

With a focus of energy and a release of intention, black energy formed around me, shimmering the air around my body. He raised an eyebrow and attacked, lunging forward with a horizontal slash.

I formed a black orb of power.

He brought the knife near my face and flicked it, but not before I released the orb in his direction. It slammed into his chest. He rolled with the blast of energy and came to his feet several feet away.

I had let him get too close.

I should have blasted him across the room immediately.

He sheathed his blade, gave me a grim smile and stepped back—out of range of my attacks.

"Not overwhelming force and no longer deepcloaked," he said, shaking his head. "You are now dead as the Mage Directorate closes in on you and proceeds to strip you of power and finally your life."

"What are you talking about?" I demanded. "I kept my mask up."

He pointed to the nearby mirror with a finger.

"Really?" he asked. "Think again. The moment you saw my blade, your focus slipped from your deepcloak to the blade I held. It's not the weapon you need to focus on, but the wielder of the weapon. You let your attention waver when you unleashed your power. I believe that's called a mortal error in technical terms."

"What are you talking about?" I asked. "I scored a clean blow on you."

"And you would be ahead on points," he said. "Bravo."

I nodded with satisfaction.

Then he showed me the strands of hair he held.

They were bright white.

My bright white strands of hair.

"No," I said, grabbing my hair with my free hand, and heading to the mirror, "I was cloaked."

"Not enough," he said. "I'm not teaching you how to spar or score points. I'm teaching you how to fight and win. You need to be the one walking away, not looking up from the ground, wondering what happened as your life pours out of you onto the cold street."

"How did I lose my deepcloak?"

"You lost your focus," he said. "You allowed it to be diverted."

"Damn it," I said under my breath.

"Congratulations, you scored one point on me, and you

will take that point with you to your death," he said. "Is that what your life is worth? A point."

"No," I said, turning to the mirror as I seethed at my narrow-minded arrogance. "You know it's not."

"Judge your opponent by their actions, not their words," he said. "Your actions showed me that."

He pointed at the mirror again.

I looked at where he pointed.

Staring back at me, my reflection was unchanged except for the bright white strands of hair on one side of my head. He was right. I had dropped my cloak. My power had raced unchecked through my body, transforming my hair and revealing who I was.

What I was.

A darkmage.

SIX

I sheathed my blade and checked my anger.

I wasn't angry at Fen.

He was one of the best instructors I could ever have, if not *the* best. No, I was angry at myself for ever thinking I could pull this off.

"This is impossible," I said, pointing at my hair. "Look at this! I'm dead. No other mage hair does this. Only darkmage hair does this."

"No, it's not impossible," he said as I grabbed my now totally white hair. "Difficult, incredibly difficult, but not impossible."

"You're dreaming if you think I can keep it together with the Directorate if I can't even maintain focus with you," I snapped. "And I've known you all of my life. I can't do this."

"I know you can," he said gently. "You are more than ready."

"Not if I can't keep my hair from turning."

"Knowing the consequences will keep you sharp," he said. "What is at the root of every mage death?"

"Complacency," I said, knowing the answer since I was a

young girl. "They overlook the details and become lax, making fatal errors."

"Overestimation and underestimation," he said. "You can exploit both."

"Present weakness when strong and strength when weak."

"Exactly, which is why we train," he said, pointing to my hair. "Restore the camouflage."

I took a deep breath and let it out slowly, letting power flow into my hand as I ran it through my hair, turning the white hair back to jet black.

The fact that my power turned all my hair white was still a mystery. It was unheard of for Darkmage hair discoloration to be so pronounced or widespread. Usually, a white patch of hair appeared over time, but could easily be hidden.

For so much of my hair to transform so suddenly as a result of my power didn't have an explanation—except to mark me as a Darkmage. Fen had told me it had always been this way, even when I was a young girl.

No other mage classification had this hair discoloration trait.

It was the way darkmages were hunted.

Hunted and killed.

Fen shook his head.

I knew where he was going and held my breath, keeping my expression neutral. As much as I hated this conversation, I deserved it, so I kept my mouth shut and looked into his yellow eyes when he exhaled, running a hand through his thick hair.

"Tell me what happens if you can't do this," he said, starting at the familiar place. "What will the Directorate do?"

"Escalate and finalize the purge."

"Don't dress it up," he said, his voice rough as he pointed a finger at me. "What does that mean?"

"Hunt down and kill every darkmage they can find."

"Everyone will be found and eliminated," he said. "Who's going to stop them?"

I looked away for a brief moment.

We had been having variations of this conversation for as long as I could remember.

"No one," I said, giving him the expected answer. "No one can."

"No, wrong," he said, knocking me off-balance with his response. "I will stop them. There are others like me walking the shadows, who will stand against the Directorate, if we must."

"What?" I asked, confused. "*You*? What others? You've never mentioned others. You can't stand against the Directorate, they'll kill you."

"I'm not *that* easy to kill," he said. "Besides, I used to be a Guardian—a Directorate Guardian. I still have some tricks left."

Something he said stayed with me.

"What others?" I asked. "You said others, what others?"

"Are you sure you want to know?"

"Yes. Tell me."

"You first," he said. "Why does the Directorate exist?"

"They are the first and last line of defense for the magical community against the nonmages," I said with a wince as he growled at me. He hated that word. "Against the non-magical communities."

"That is what they *were*, long ago, before you walked this earth," he said with a nod. "Tell me why they exist *now*. What is the purpose of the Pentarch and the Directorate?"

"The Directorate polices the magical community," I said. "The Pentarch controls the Directorate. They keep mages and the magical community in check, controlling them when they can, killing them when they can't."

"That's closer to the truth," he said. "What do they perceive as their greatest threat?"

"Darkmages."

"Wrong," Fen said, surprising me again. "I said what do they *perceive* as their greatest threat, not what *is* their greatest threat. Try again and this time give it some thought. Answer without letting emotion cloud your thought process. What do they perceive as the greatest threat to the Mage Directorate?"

I gave it some thought.

The Directorate was a vast organization, spanning the world.

Even with their size, they still weren't large enough to control all of the mages on the planet.

The magical community was immense, but splintered, with no one knowing its true size, or how far it reached. Mages and those who possessed abilities were secretive by nature, preferring to live in the shadows.

There had been talk once of the Mage Directorate conducting a worldwide magical census. The pretense was: how could the needs of the magical community be met if their numbers were unknown?

With a census, those who needed the most help could be identified and assisted. Many saw it for what it was—a power move disguised with a lie, designed to establish the Directorate's authority and exert pressure on the magical community to comply.

The Directorate underestimated the loosely organized magical community; the census idea was met with violence. So much so, that the Directorate had to pull back and reconsider the idea—for now.

I doubted they had shelved it permanently.

If there was one thing people with power craved above everything else, it was more power. Since they weren't able to identify all of the magic users, the only way to keep their power was to keep mages in fear.

They needed to keep mages in check. If mages ever truly organized, the Directorate would never stand a chance.

For that, they used fear, intimidation, and the advantage of anonymity, with the most powerful mages in the Pentarch and the Directorate moving in the shadows—their identities hidden from the rest.

It came to me suddenly.

"Control," I said as Fen nodded. "They fear losing control over the power they possess."

"How do they maintain this control?"

"They've created a scapegoat, a target to keep the mages in fear," I said as the anger began to rise within. "A group to *other*, to blame for everything that goes wrong in the magical community."

Fen nodded.

"Keep your rage in check," Fen warned. "You have every right to feel angry. You have no right to lose control...not yet. Who is this group?"

"Me," I said, seething. "The darkmages."

"Again," he said patiently, "you have every right to your anger, but if you let it cloud your reason, you will become just another statistic who couldn't hold it together when she confronted the Hounds. Get your rage under control and *keep* it under control. Who is this group?"

"Darkmages," I said the word like the curse it was. "The darkmages."

"Why them?" Fen asked, grabbing his mug of coffee again. "Why target all the darkmages?"

It was the same question that had stolen my sleep many nights when I was younger. Every time I heard the stories of darkmages being erased, or accused of horrific crimes and executed without mercy. Every time darkmages were called evil and worthy of death, their only crime being they existed.

Every time I asked Fen, he would say the same thing: people fear what they don't understand.

Even mages.

Especially mages.

Fen would tell me they hated me because I was special, because my power was different from theirs.

It was so different it scared them into taking the only action they understood. I needed to be eliminated, erased from existence. That would be the only way they could sleep at night, safe and secure in the knowledge that the threat I presented, the threat that darkmages presented, was gone.

SEVEN

Somehow, his last question stayed with me. Something about the way he asked it seemed off in my head.

"Hold on," I said, slowly piecing it together. "Not *all* the darkmages. The Directorate has a specific focus on the Forzas, my family. Specifically, *my* family."

"Why?" Fen asked gently. "Why *your* family?"

"Aside from the fact that my grandfather is a homicidal maniac that has killed thousands of Directorate mages?"

Fen nodded, his expression grim.

"He has kept busy, but yes, aside from that," Fen said. "He's a threat, but there is a greater threat related to your family."

"The Eclipse," I said, seeing the connection. "This is about the Eclipse."

"What about it?"

"The bloodline," I said as it finally fell into place. "Only the bloodline can wield The Eclipse."

"That blade is the greatest threat to the Directorate," he said. "If they can't find the Eclipse, what would be the best way to neutralize the threat?"

"The next best thing—destroy the bloodline," I said. "That would eliminate the greatest threat to the Directorate. That way no one could use the sword."

"If they can't have one, they can eliminate the other."

"If I give them the blade, you think they would take my word that I'll leave them alone?" I asked. "I'll convince them I'm *retired*."

"They would only believe that under a very specific set of circumstances," he said. "Which are?"

"First, I have to actually *find* the Eclipse."

"That would help, which would then prompt the Directorate to...?"

"Erase and then kill me, though I don't think they will be picky about the order."

"With extreme prejudice," he said. "What else happens if you give the Directorate the Eclipse? What would that trigger?"

"War," I said. "Too many people, mages, especially darkmages, would declare war on the Directorate. With the Eclipse they would finally be able to stand against the Directorate."

"Can't they stand against the Directorate now?"

"Actually, yes," Fen said. "If they organized and formed a cohesive enclave of darkmages. That would be fearsome to face. It's fearsome to consider."

"Why don't they?"

"The Directorate's misinformation campaign has been incredibly successful," he said with a small head shake. "Darkmages don't trust other mages; they barely trust each other. They are a fractured group within the splintered magical community. But if they had a leader and a weapon to rally behind..."

"They would unite," I said, seeing where Fen was going. "It would get bloody fast."

"The moment you declare yourself *retired* and surrender to the Directorate, giving them the Eclipse, I can assure you that if your grandfather *is* alive, he will begin his comeback tour."

"That would be nightmarish for everyone involved."

Fen nodded.

"What would be his first stop?" he asked. "Where would the blood begin to flow first?"

"Wherever the Eclipse was being held," I said. "Do you really think he would come back? He's been gone for so long."

"Not gone. Waiting," Fen replied. "He has time. Some of my sources have strong evidence that he's still alive. He never remains in one place for too long, but they assure me it's him."

"How can you be so sure?" I asked, hoping against hope that they were wrong. "Maybe they made a mistake? Maybe it was someone who looked like him?"

"It's possible. Energy signatures can be masked, but they can't be altered. There's an excellent chance it's him—enough of one that I wouldn't bury him just yet."

"Why can't the Directorate secure the Eclipse?" I asked. "They can put it in some special vault or something, someplace ultra-secure where he could never get to it."

"His power increases in proximity to the blade," Fen said. "Not even a null space can negate that effect of the Eclipse. Once it's in his hands, he's nearly unstoppable."

"They did it once," I said, my voice low. "How did they stop him last time?"

"That wasn't the Directorate," Fen said. "Even their strongest mage could never face your grandfather. No, that was someone else."

"Someone who worked for the Directorate?"

"Someone who worked *with* the Directorate," he said.

"There's a vast difference between the two. You're referring to Archon Quinn."

"Quinn was the only mage to face my grandfather and beat him."

"He killed Archon Quinn for that—the last Directorate mage who managed to fight him to a standstill," Fen said. "Only Quinn—another darkmage—was able to stand against your grandfather. No one knows what he did, only that he managed to wound your grandfather enough to take the Eclipse, securing it within the Directorate. He paid for that move with his life."

"Why won't they admit that they still have the Eclipse?"

"No one currently knows where the Eclipse is," he said. "The rumors are that Archon Quinn sealed it in a void, and no one can get to it."

"Aren't there any mages strong enough to find and access this void?"

"That would require a particular type of Archon."

"A *darkmage* Archon," I said, understanding how impossible that was. "The Directorate has made *that* nearly impossible."

"Agreed," Fen said. "Their animosity toward and persecution of darkmages makes another darkmage Archon improbable in this current climate."

"Improbable? More like impossible."

"You'd think the Directorate would attempt a different method," he said. "It's either find your grandfather, someone from his lineage, or train a darkmage to become strong enough to access the Eclipse."

"Is that why...no, that would be crazy," I said, shaking my head. "They wouldn't go through all that trouble just to find—?"

"What?" Fen said serious. "Share, even if it sounds crazy."

"The whole reason they're targeting darkmages is to

create another Archon who can access and locate the Eclipse," I said. "I mean they have to have the information somewhere, even if they can't access the sword itself."

"An Archon is a highly specialized elite mage," Fen said. "If they need someone powerful to wield the Eclipse, a mage has to undergo the ascension, becoming an Archon. It would require a near fatal transformation. In this case, a darkmage would need to perform the ascension ritual and transcend to Archon."

"It sounds out there," I said. "But maybe that's what the Directorate is doing?"

"You're not the only one who holds that theory," Fen said. "It's not out of the realm of possibility and fits with the other rumor."

"What other rumor?"

"This one hasn't been corroborated, but it makes sense."

"What does?"

"Quinn's staff—Brightshadow was never recovered from the debris of that final battle. The rumor is that the Eclipse was shattered into five sections during that final battle, and the Directorate only recovered a piece of the sword, not the entire blade."

"Is that possible?"

"Quinn could've used Brightshadow as a key to create an interstice," he said. "There, he could have stored parts of Eclipse, if it was broken. Like a sort of secured space."

"They would never admit to something like that," I said realizing the depth of the subterfuge if true. "It would completely undermine the strength the Directorate tries to project."

"Not the sort of thing you broadcast, no."

"But that means they would know where the rest of the Eclipse is—that would be—"

"Closely guarded information," Fen said. "So close in fact,

that it could easily cost someone their life. It would be information the Directorate couldn't act on, but that would hold tremendous value."

"Why not?" I asked. "They have the location."

"Brightshadow is a darkmage weapon."

"That means they're back to square one," I said, seeing the problem. "They still need a darkmage Archon to even get near Brightshadow. It's like having the key to a door you know exists, but it's hidden and you can't find it."

He nodded.

"Which means the Pentarch and the Directorate are?"

"Anxious to unlock that door and get their hands on that sword."

"Homicidally so," he said. "The second part of that rumor is that somehow Quinn managed to use his staff as an anchor to keep the rest of the Eclipse in its shattered state—in stasis."

"Stasis?" I asked. "Are you sure?"

"As far as anything about that sword can be certain —yes."

"If it's in stasis, the Directorate will *never* be able to access the Eclipse without a darkmage. If any other mage tries—it's a suicide attempt."

"It's only a rumor, mind you," Fen said. "Mostly unfounded hearsay."

"It contains an odd amount of detail for being just a rumor," I said. "Who told you all of this?"

"I can't say," he answered. "But in every rumor, I feel there is a kernel of truth. In this case, it's just hard to determine what's truth or fiction."

"That's why I'm going in?"

"That's why you're going in *and* making sure you come out again," he said. "The Mage Directorate has not been able to fill the position of Archon since Quinn. I have to imagine his staff is somewhere in Directorate HQ in some secure location—"

"That they can't access," I said with a grim smile. "It must be driving the Lead Mages insane—I love it."

"You need to be careful with that glee," Fen said. "The current Lead Mage—Emery, has made it his life's mission to find the Eclipse, or make sure no one can ever wield it."

"He can't locate that sword," I said in disbelief. "Is he insane? If the sword reappears..."

"No security or defensive wards would keep your grandfather out," Fen said. "He would cut through them all to get his blade back. And then?"

"The massacre," I said, my voice low. "He would kill them all."

"All of them," Fen said, his voice somber. "As bad as the Directorate is, and it's plenty bad, having your grandfather take control of the Eclipse again, is orders of magnitude worse."

"Can't we just destroy it?"

"The Directorate?" he asked. "It's been tried; they're worse than roaches. They keep coming back."

"You know what I mean," I said, exasperated. "The Eclipse. Why can't we just destroy it? I mean Quinn managed to break it."

"Allegedly, and that cost him his life," he said. "You want the short answer?"

"If you'd be so kind."

"Destroying the Eclipse is nearly impossible."

"That's hard to believe," I said. "If it was created, it can be unmade."

"The Eclipse is a unique blade," he said. "It's a hardlight blade."

"A hardlight blade?" I asked. "What does that even mean?"

"Look, unmaking that blade would put the entire plane at

risk," Fen said, looking off to the side. "The method of forging the Eclipse...it's not an ordinary blade. Darkmage magic was used to harness the power of a neutron star, and the way to do that has been lost to time. The rumor is that there is so much power contained within that blade, that to unmake it is to unmake the world."

"The power of a star?" I said, raising an eyebrow. "Inside a sword, really?"

"I wasn't there when it was made," he said. "That is the rumor around its forging."

"Another rumor? You do realize that sounds like a load of BS, right?" I said. "Something alleged to keep the curious satisfied. Or those who are easily swayed by fairy tales of super mystical swords of power. You're placing a lot of faith in rumors lately."

"Hey, there was a time when my kind were considered rumor and fairy tales," he said. "I won't even go into what darkmages were considered to be—they were the stuff of nightmares—so yes, maybe it's heavy on the rumor, but in these cases, the rumors mask the truth most of the time."

"And you believe the rumors about the Eclipse?" I said, touching the ring that hung around my neck. "You think they're true?"

"I do. Normally I wouldn't, except that I have seen that blade in action, twice," Fen said. "Both times, what it did could not be explained. It sundered reality itself. Trust me, no one is going to take a chance destroying *that* blade."

"So I'm stuck."

"For now, it means more training until you maintain uninterrupted focus," he said. "What are the disciplines?"

"Wood, Igneous, Terra, Aqua, Metal," I said, reciting the order from memory. "Interactions?"

"If you would be so kind," he said, moving into a defensive stance. "Start with Wood."

"Wood depletes Terra, Terra obstructs Aqua, Aqua extinguishes Igneous, Igneous vaporizes Metal, Metal destroys Wood."

"What is the unspoken discipline?"

"Stasis," I said. "The discipline of the darkmages."

"What does stasis counteract?"

"Everything," I said. "Stasis negates all. It holds everything and nothing."

"Remember that *always*," he said, his voice somber. "It's the deepest fear of the Pentarch and the true reason the Directorate hunt and kill darkmages. They are vulnerable to stasis, which is why they feared your grandfather and his blade."

"What can I possibly do alone?" I asked. "I'm just one person against the entire Directorate?"

"From the outside, very little," he said. "From within? Even the greatest defense can be brought down from within. This is why we train, to enhance your focus and prepare you while there is time."

"Or until the Directorate finds me."

"Let's make sure that doesn't happen...until we're ready," he said, stepping back and showing me his hands. "Get ready."

I bowed and stepped into a defensive stance.

"Ready."

"Good," he said. "No weapons this time. Attack."

EIGHT

Fen had been unrelenting in the unarmed portion of my torture disguised as training, and had worked up a thirst from the 'pounding my head with his hands' practice.

He had bounced me all over the floor of our training space until the sun peeked over the horizon. We ended the session with my body bruised and battered.

Once, when we were done, he had declared me nearly ready. All I needed was a few more decades of focused practice before he could trust me to infiltrate what he considered hostile territory.

I knew he was joking.

It was his backhanded way of giving me a compliment. He never told me outright that I did well. It was always: I needed a few more decades before he could consider me ready.

Except that each training session became more and more brutal. We had been at this for years, and I knew—because he had said it himself—it was time to unleash me on the Directorate.

I liked that description, because I always compared it to

being a force of nature that was unleashed on an unsuspecting group of myopic mages bent on destroying my kind, and me tearing them apart.

Fine. I had some pent-up anger issues regarding the Directorate.

It was after these training sessions that Fen would say cryptic things like: *I wish he would show up already* or *When is the furry bugger going to show his face?*

I never knew who he referred to in these comments, and he would change the subject when I pressed him, so I learned to be patient regarding whoever this 'furry bugger' was.

I vaguely remembered a conversation about a second Guardian on the day I had arrived at what was now my home. The man—the Traveler, as Fen called him—had mentioned a second Guardian. Whenever I brought it up to Fen, he said I would know when it happened.

Then he ended the conversation.

I hadn't forgotten, though.

I had a feeling he was waiting for this *bugger* to show up before sending me to the Directorate. What if he never showed up? Did that mean Fen would wait before sending me to the Directorate?

"You're going to send me soon, aren't you?"

He wiped the sweat from his face and gave me a look.

"What makes you say that?"

"Aside from the fact that my training sessions can be described as attempted murder, you mean?"

"I need to make sure you're ready," he said. "Your power is still mostly dormant."

"I see," I said, wiping my face with a towel. "Your strategy is to take me to the brink of death to see if my powers manifest? Is that your training method?"

"If the Directorate finds out the truth about you, do you think they will just have a conversation with you?" he asked as he tossed his towel over his shoulder. "What do you think will happen?"

"I won't let that happen," I said. "I'm ready. My cover is nearly perfect."

He laughed and shook his head.

"You're ready when I say you're ready," he said. "You can't even hold your own against me. The Directorate Enforcers will eat you alive. It will be sooner than you expect. Trust the process."

This meant he was going to send me into the Directorate soon, probably sooner than he wanted to.

I knew he didn't want to, but the Directorate had increased their attacks against darkmages and were still looking for the Eclipse. I decided to flank him and attack from a different angle.

"Are you waiting for the *furry bugger*?"

"The what?" he said surprised. "There's no furry bugger."

"You keep mentioning a furry bugger and wondering when he's going to show up," I said matter-of-factly. "I figured you were waiting for him to show up before you sent me to the Directorate. Is that what this is?"

"You have no idea what you're talking about," he said, looking away, using his deflection face. "It's just an expression I use."

"Lie," I said. "That was a lie. You can't lie to me. You always do that thing with your eye when you lie."

"What thing?" he said, looking at me. "Did I hit your head too hard?"

"*You* taught me how to look for tics and tells," I said, pointing at him. "Your eye squints—just your left one—whenever you say something that is either questionable or an outright lie. Never fails." I pointed to my left eye. "Every time."

"I have no such tell," he protested. "You're imagining

things. Why don't you go change. We have a tactics class after breakfast. And you need to get some more milk."

"More milk? You went through that gallon I got you this morning?"

"A gallon is me just getting started," he said with a grin. "Besides this will give you masking practice. Your last milk run your masking was a disaster."

"Fine," I said. "Why don't I bring back a cow? That would solve your milk issues."

"Could you?" he said. "It would be appreciated."

"Hilarious," I muttered as I walked away. "Beats me to a pulp, then sends me for milk."

"I heard that," he said as I headed for the stairs. "Don't get me none of the two percent milk water either."

I shook my head.

His hearing was beyond sharp. Milk was his preferred drink and he ran through gallons of it like water. When I was younger, the amount of milk he consumed astounded me.

Our current conversation brought a smile to my face as I prepped to go downstairs.

"You know, you could drink this other amazing drink," I called out. "It's called water. Ever hear of it?"

"Bah, bland and tasteless," he complained. "Milk makes my bones strong. It does a body good." He flexed a bicep. "Look at these cannons."

"It's guns, and why don't we just get a few cows?" I suggested. "That way you can milk them and have a never-ending supply of your favorite drink?"

"Too much upkeep," he answered. "If we had a farm..."

"No farms," I said quickly. "I am not living on another farm ever again. Ever."

Once, when Fen feared the Directorate was getting too close, we had briefly stayed at a farm in the Finger Lakes region, away from the city for a time. He had moved us there temporarily, promising it would be a good change for me.

He was wrong.

"It's quiet and we can have cows, maybe some pigs," he tried unconvincingly. "C'mon you loved the farm."

I poked my head back into the training room and stared daggers at him.

"I hated the farm and you know it," I snapped back. "It was always dirty and cold or unbearably hot. Farm life is torture."

"Farm life made you strong," he said. "Farm life is preferable to living in this concrete jungle."

"You know what I love about the city?" I asked. "No animals."

"You are mistaken," he said, his voice serious. "There are still animals, dangerous ones in fact. They just walk on two legs now."

"I'll take them over the four legged ones that hated me."

"You never learned to control your energy around them," he said. "You constantly spooked them."

"Which is why we will never have animals or live on a farm."

"I loved the farm," he said wistfully. "Quiet life away from the Directorate and their Hounds."

"No place is safe from them now," I said. "You taught me that."

"I did," he said, waving me off. "Be careful out there. Eyes?"

"360 on a swivel."

"Focus?"

"Everywhere and nowhere."

"Energy signature?"

"Under control and invisible."

"Good," he said with a nod. "Get three gallons this time and come straight back. There's been heightened Directorate activity in the area in addition to their regular patrols, as of late. No sense in being out more than you need to."

I took the stairs down to the ground floor.

NINE

I could hear the strain in his voice.

It was nearly impossible to detect, but I had spent most of my life listening to his voice, studying it for inflections and nuances. He had trained me to be the best, even better than he was.

He was nervous for me, probably more nervous than I was. To be honest, I felt I was more than ready. I had nearly perfected my ice mage cover, masking the null aspects of my energy signature. Not even Fen could tell I was a darkmage.

My power had not fully manifested, but I knew it would soon. Until then, I could use ice like any other ice mage. Stasis would be another thing entirely.

If I unleashed that power, I would be discovered immediately. Stasis wasn't subtle. It was all about destruction and devastation. There was a reason darkmages were feared. A darkmage wielded more power than any mage from any of the other disciplines because darkmages drew their power directly from the energy around them, tapping into the source.

If my power manifested without a teacher to help me

control it, the Directorate would find and erase me. In order to control my stasis ability, I needed a darkmage instructor.

Fen wasn't a darkmage.

I absentmindedly ran a finger along the edge of my ring. The dark energy inside of it hummed at my touch, resonating with the power within.

Eventually, I knew I would need an actual darkmage when my power did manifest. I would need instruction and guidance, things Fen couldn't show me. Manifesting while I was in the Directorate would be a problem.

A problem that could get me killed.

The only saving grace was that darkmage power and ice mage abilities were close in energy signature. It was theorized that ice mages were simply unmanifested darkmages. No one had proven that theory, but ice mages were rare and distrusted.

I glanced down at the ring between my fingers.

The ring was my failsafe to prevent noticeable outward demonstrations of my stasis power, but I didn't know how effective it would be if I lost control and let my hair turn completely, or something worse, like a spontaneous blast of dark magic. If that happened, it was all over.

They would exterminate me on sight.

The Directorate Enforcers would crush me before I had a chance to react. I had to trust my failsafes and hope I could deal with my stasis ability when it happened. It made no sense to worry about things I couldn't control.

Fen's words came back to me: *Don't let the things you can't control, control you.*

I took a moment to catch my breath as I left our home. There was always a moment of hesitation before I stepped outside. We were currently living at 41 Commerce Street, on the corner of Commerce and Barrow Streets, in a converted townhouse.

All three floors belonged to us, with the ground floor and second floor for living, and the third floor for training. I opened the door and immediately felt the aura of power from the wards around the house envelope me, masking my energy signature.

The ring acted as an extension of the mask. I could travel several blocks away and still maintain the mask. If I went too far from the house, I risked breaking the connection and being exposed.

In essence, the ring hid me in plain sight. Fen said it was important for me to get out and move in the world, but not to be noticed.

That was his explanation for sending me on these short runs to several locations. I always had the feeling he was shadowing me to make sure I didn't get lost.

I never once caught him following me, but I always felt he was close by.

I had no idea how he expected me to infiltrate the Mage Directorate. Even with my ice mage disguise, the Directorate Apprentice initiation process was grueling and extremely selective.

It was true, he had trained me in subterfuge, combat, tactics, and how to mask my ability, but as I had kept demonstrating over and over, holding that mask in the face of danger was proving to be an impossible challenge.

There was no way I could pass the entrance selection process, not without giving away my true identity. I needed another way in or this plan was over before it began.

I shook my head as I let the plan run through my mind.

It was impossible.

"Difficult, not impossible," I said to myself as I walked the few blocks back to Patricia's deli. "Practice, Val. That's how it's going to happen. Unending grinding and mind-numbing practice."

I had walked for several blocks before a surge of power stopped me suddenly. I felt the surge of energy before I saw it.

My heart raced as the power grew closer.

Mages. There were mages close by. I sensed the energy and felt for its source. These weren't just any mages. I recognized the power, and fear gripped me.

Directorate Mages.

I had only sensed this type of power once before, when I was a child. I looked around, but saw nothing. What did surprise me was that I saw no one on the streets around me. The street was empty.

I grabbed my ring and fed power into it, just enough to activate my mask, but not enough to attract attention from any wandering Directorate Mages.

"That's odd," I muttered to myself as I kept looking around. "I know it's early, but these streets are rarely this empty."

The surge of power increased behind me.

I dashed to the nearest wall and squeezed my body flat against it the way Fen had trained me so many times.

I managed to turn in time to see the fireball blaze past my face. The intensity of the fireball surprised me. Even though I had sensed it, I wasn't prepared for the heat that nearly insta-tanned my face.

I followed the bright orange-red fireball with my gaze.

It crashed into an unknown man, detonating with a loud *thwump* as all the oxygen in the immediate area around him was consumed.

It had been so fast I hadn't had time to think. I merely reacted. I pushed off the wall, bracing myself for the charred body that surely remained of the target.

Once the flames dissipated, the man stepped forward,

dusting himself off. He looked unharmed. In fact, he looked angry as red energy formed around his hands.

"What was that, Michael?" the man said. "Since when do you use warning shots?"

"Bleed me dry," I hissed under my breath as a Directorate mage closed on the man who had thrown up a shield to deflect the fireball. "He's still alive."

"Surrender," the Directorate mage ordered, and I turned at his voice. It was short, stocky and dangerous from the morning Enforcer Patrols. "That was just meant to get your attention. Reinforcements are on their way. This is futile, Eric."

Short, stocky, and dangerous was named Michael. He looked beyond livid. Whoever this Eric was, he had done something to anger him to a homicidal level.

"Surrender?" Eric said. "You must be delusional. Tell me, did you really need to kill the changeling? Or were you just letting your sadistic side out for a little air?"

"Does it matter?" Michael answered. "He went rogue, and you know the rules. Rogue changelings get the same treatment as darkmages. They get dead."

I was liking Michael less by the second.

"Of course it matters," Eric shot back, looking at a third Directorate mage who joined them. "Tell him, Xander. Tell him that changeling wasn't a threat. He didn't deserve to die."

Xander—tall, dark, and handsome—had just come around the corner, and my heart seized for a second as I took him in. He was still gorgeous, but his eyes held a dangerous glint. I had never sensed their energy signatures before. Whatever was going on was serious. They weren't patrolling. This energy signature meant they were ready for battle.

I needed to get off this street.

"For all we know, he could have been assisting the darkmage," Michael said. "Aiding and abetting a darkmage incurs the same consequence as if he had been a darkmage."

"A convenient lie," Eric said. "Is this what we've become? Murderers for the Directorate?"

Xander remained silent, but looked away, his expression a mixture of pain and anger. My brain nearly checked out as I got a better look at his chiseled jaw and well-proportioned features.

He's dangerous. He's Directorate.

I reminded myself and got myself under control.

They all wore the black and red uniform of Directorate Enforcers—a red shirt and black tie under a black business suit, reinforced with sigils of protection with a solid red band of symbols along one arm. Their faces were uncovered, which surprised me. Directorate Mages on official business usually wore helms that covered the top half of their faces— a sort of half-mask to hide their identities.

Maybe these Enforcers were from a different division. I didn't entirely recognize the uniform, but I recognized the colors.

The colors, red and black, meant they were from the Igneous discipline. Most of the Directorate Enforcers were from the same discipline.

Fen once told me it was one of the strongest and most feared of the disciplines. The Directorate preferred practitioners from the Igneous discipline because they made the most effective and deadly Enforcers.

That explained the fireball.

Xander looked at Michael, the Directorate Enforcer who had attacked, and shook his head.

"The changeling is alive," Xander said. "He barely managed to get away, along with the darkmage, but they weren't together."

"The changeling means nothing, but the darkmage—he

got away?" Michael asked, his expression irritated. "No matter, I'll find him. I'll find them both."

"He won't get far, not with that wound you gave him," Xander said. "The changeling is a lost cause. We'll never find it once it reaches a populated area. It will blend in and disappear."

"Damn it. *You* let him get away," Michael said as he turned to face Xander, the anger clear in his eyes. "I'll hunt it *and* the darkmage down, once I deal with this traitor. No one escapes the Directorate."

"Michael," Xander said, "why don't we take this back to the Directorate HQ? This situation is getting out of control and the aversion runes you cast won't work indefinitely. We'll have normals on the streets soon."

"They don't need to last indefinitely," Michael said, taking a breath and regaining his composure. "They only need to work long enough for me to deal with him."

Michael turned to glare at Eric.

I took a step back, closer to the wall.

Xander glanced at me and subtly shook his head.

How did he see me? He actually saw me?

I was worried by the fact that my mask had failed and that he had actually noticed me. If they discovered I was a darkmage, I was dead.

I couldn't believe he could see me clearly. If my mask was working properly, I should have blended into the background of the street and been overlooked.

Either this Xander was stronger than the average Enforcer, or my mask wasn't as strong as I thought.

Either way this was bad news.

"Michael, if you unleash another one of your blasts in this street, you could hurt someone," Xander said. "Someone innocent, like her."

Xander pointed at me.

"No one is innocent," Michael answered, glancing at me as if seeing me for the first time. "Haven't you learned that by now? If she gets caught in my blast, I'm not the one to blame." He motioned to Eric with his chin. "That falls on him. He was the one who led us down this street. Besides, she's a normal."

He said that last part with a tone that meant I was expendable.

"That doesn't justify her death," Xander said. "We can't just go around murdering people, just because they're normal."

"Are you insane?" Michael asked. "That's not what I meant."

"That's what it sounded like," Xander said, an edge to his voice. "What did you mean? Exactly."

"She's a normal, meaning just obscure her sight and cloud her memory." He waved a hand in my direction. "She won't see or remember anything," Michael explained. "However, you know we can't have witnesses to magical activity."

"I'm aware," Xander replied. "The Directorate has enough bad PR as it is. We don't need to add to it."

"Exactly. If you don't obscure her, she goes from innocent bystander to collateral damage." He turned to Eric. "Either way, it's not my problem; her blood will be on your hands, Eric. I'm just following orders."

"Said every coward of a killer in history," Eric scoffed. "That how you dress it up so you can sleep at night? You're just following orders?"

"Unlike you, I'm not *confused*, Eric," Michael snarled. "I took an oath, we *all* did. We all swore to uphold that oath on pain of death, or did you forget?"

"I didn't forget."

"Then what is the issue? Either Xander obscures and clouds her, or she has to be removed permanently," Michael answered. "This is SOP. Are you upset because of a dead changeling? Seriously?" He turned to Xander. "Xander? Can you do it or not?"

"She didn't ask to be in the middle of this," Xander said with a nod. "I can obscure her. I got it."

"Make sure it takes," Michael answered without even glancing at me. "Don't forget the memory cloud."

"It'll work," Xander said. "Just give me a minute."

Xander stepped close to me and gestured, releasing some golden runic symbols into the air. I could barely focus on the symbols as my vision was locked on his face.

Wake the hell up, you're in danger!

The symbols slowly descended on me, blurring my vision for a few seconds, before everything became clear again. He gestured again, and a darker set of symbols floated over to where I stood, buzzing in my head as they impacted me.

I had an idea what the symbols were meant to do, but I felt the power of my ring hum on my chest. Whatever was supposed to happen, my ring had blocked the effect of the casts. I could see everything clearly and my memory was intact.

"Done?" Michael asked. "Did it work?"

"As far as I can tell, yes," Xander said, looking deep into my eyes as he placed a hand on either side of my face and pulled me close to peer into my eyes. We were nearly close enough to kiss. "The obscuring is in place and the memory cloud will take effect in a few minutes. She won't remember or be able to see anything important."

"I hope so, for her sake, Xan," Michael answered. "You can't save everyone. I would hate to have to cleanse her, but rules are rules. We have our orders."

"And you're just following orders, is that it?" Eric said from behind a shield of energy. "Always the good little soldier. You're just a pawn like all the others. Have you ever stopped to consider why the Pentarch wants darkmages dead?"

I realized Enforcer Michael was somewhat unstable in a dangerously homicidal way. He didn't care about anyone who wasn't a mage, and even then, he only cared for those who seemed to believe as he did.

He seemed to be the leader of this group, and as the leader, he was used to being listened to and having his orders followed without question.

This was getting worse by the moment.

If I tried to leave, there was a good chance he would lash out and hit me with one of those fireballs. If I stayed, the chances of getting caught up in this mage battle increased by the second.

"I have," Michael said after a pause. "It's because darkmages are a threat to everything we stand for. They corrupt everything and everyone they touch with their lies and deceptions. The way they corrupted you."

The dormant rage inside of me reared its head, but I kept it under control. According to them, I was a normal—I wouldn't know about darkmages, or the Directorate hunting and killing us just because we were different.

"You're wrong," Eric countered, surprising me. It took all the strength of will I possessed to keep my expression neutral. He was an Enforcer, but he believed darkmages deserved a chance. He had just sentenced himself to death. "Darkmages are not evil. They're people just like us, with hopes and dreams. They only want to be able to live in peace, left alone to live their lives. They pose us no threat. Darkmages—"

"No," Michael said, his voice a blade of finality, cutting him off. "Darkmages die, everyone knows this. I know this. You *know* this. It has been this way since the Directorate was created."

I felt the subtle increase in power around me. All three of these mages were gathering power into themselves. The air in the street all around us was becoming charged with energy.

I looked around and ducked back into one of the nearby doorways to present the smallest target possible. This was going to be a magical battle in broad daylight. They were either monumentally stupid, insane, or both. Once they got started, it would attract all kinds of attention.

None of it good.

It didn't matter what kind of aversion runes were in place, a magical battle in the heart of the Village in the middle of the morning would get noticed by the Directorate and the population of the neighborhood.

That's when things would really get ugly.

I needed to be gone before that happened.

TEN

"Of course I *know* this," Eric snapped. "I wanted...I needed to know *why*? Why do darkmages die? Why can't the Directorate answer that simple question? What are they so scared of? Have you ever met or spoken to a darkmage?"

"Darkmages are a danger not only to themselves, but to society as we know it, and to the entire Directorate," Michael said. "Speak to them? Are you *insane*? What for? They are a blight on society, worthy only of extermination."

"I've spoken to them," Eric said, lowering his voice. "They're people, not monsters."

Michael turned his face away.

"Look at me," Eric continued. "Do I look tainted? Look at me. It's still me, your Directorate brother. We trained together, fought together, and now, because I spoke to a darkmage, I'm corrupted? Am I evil? The Pentarch are wrong. You *know* they're wrong."

"We don't question the Pentarch...ever," Michael answered, his voice steel. "Especially when it comes to darkmages. They know of what they speak. They're older and wiser than we will ever be."

"Exactly what they taught you to say," Eric scoffed. "Do you ever plan on having an original thought? You don't have to believe everything they say. You're allowed to have a free will."

"You should have never met with darkmages," Michael said, regret in his voice. "They confused you. Corrupted your mind with their ideas. It's what they do. You let them get to you."

"Stop this," Xander said. I noticed he had moved closer to where I stood. "We don't need to do this. We can resolve this back at the Directorate."

Michael shook his head.

"Eric chose to resolve this here and now," Michael said. "He's choosing that scum darkmage over us, over his family, over the Directorate. Isn't that right, Eric?"

"You've always been too trusting," Eric said, drawing red energy into his hands. "You've always believed them. The Pentarch lied to us, lies to us still."

"What are you doing?" Xander asked, surprised, looking from Michael to Eric. "Both of you, stop this. We are all Enforcers, brothers. We all belong to the Directorate."

"Eric, you're my brother so I'm giving you a choice today," Michael said, ignoring Xander. "Today, you're going to choose between your brothers, your oath and your duty, or a worthless darkmage and a changeling."

"Don't do this, Eric," Xander said. "Come back with us. We can get you help. The darkmages just confused you. You can be helped, it's not too late."

"Can't you see? He's beyond help, Xan," Michael said, never taking his eyes off Eric. "He's turned his back on us, on the Directorate."

"No," Xander said, shaking his head. "Cease and desist, Eric. Michael doesn't really want to hurt you. Don't do this;

you can't hope to match his ability. He's stronger than you and me combined, you know this."

"Actually, I *do* want to hurt him," Michael said. "He prefers darkmages over us? Fine. He can breathe his last with them, too."

"Surrender and come back, Eric," Xander pleaded. "We can help you. You're just confused. Whatever the darkmage told you was a lie. Let the Pentarchs help you."

Eric smiled a sad smile and formed an orb of black and red energy. I stepped farther away from Xander, angling my body to exit the street once the orbs of magic started flying.

"Help me?" Eric said. "How? By erasing me? Stripping me of all power? No, thanks, I *refuse* your idea of *help*."

"You know the darkmages are evil," Xander said. "You know—"

"No," Eric said, shaking his head as he looked down at the orb in his hand. "Those are lies. Lies I used to believe, just like you two do. They aren't evil. *We* are the villains in their story. We are the ones that hunt them down—"

"Because they are dangerous," Michael finished. "Because they're ruthless, cold-blooded killers who show no mercy to their enemies."

"No!" Eric yelled. "Because they are powerful. The Directorate *fears* them. They won't be good little sheep and so the Directorate feels the need to wipe them out. Can't you see it? Darkmages threaten the Directorate's control."

"All I see is my brother who needs help," Xander said. "Let us help you. Come back. We can help you."

"You can't save him, Ashford," Michael said. "Xan, he's too far gone."

So, his name was Xander Ashford. Maybe Fen could get more information on him and his role in the Directorate Enforcers.

"No one can help me now," Eric said with a short, humorless laugh. "Once those reinforcements arrive, I'll be executed on sight."

"I won't let them," Xander said. "I can stop them."

"No, you can't, brother," Eric said, looking up. "They're close now. They won't listen to you. They have an Inquisitor with them."

Eric hefted the black and red orb in his hand as he focused on Michael again.

"Please, Eric," Xander said. "Don't do this. Stand down. You're confused."

"No, Xan, for the very first time in a long time, I can see clearly."

"No, you're not seeing clearly," Xander countered. "They've blinded you to the truth, this is what darkmages do. They fill your head with lies, turn you against your family, against everything you stand for."

"I feel sorry for you, Xander," Eric said. "You're too soft to be a Directorate Enforcer. You keep doing this, and it's going to get you killed...just like me. They're going to send you out one day, and your target is going to be...inconvenient."

"Don't," Xander said. "Stop the orb. Stand down."

"Your target is going to be some darkmage or someone else the Pentarchs deem dangerous, like an Enforcer gone rogue," Eric continued with a sad smile. "You're going to start asking questions. One day, you're going to ask the right questions around the wrong people. Then the next target for cleansing will be...you."

"Don't do this," Xander said relentlessly. "You can come back. Come back!"

"Here's your choice," Eric said, holding up the orb, ignoring Xander and looking at Michael. "There's no coming back from this one."

"Eric, no!"

"Let him go, Xan," Michael said, facing Eric and stepping into the street across from him. "He's made his choice."

"I have," Eric said. "Xan is too soft for this, but I know *you* can do it, Michael. I invoke the choice of the final rite."

Michael nodded as more energy flowed into his hands.

"Offer your choice," Michael said, his voice hard. "Ashford...Xan, don't interfere in this. He's invoked his final rite."

"Don't throw your life away," Xan said.

"You're going to have to kill me, let me go, or die," Eric continued, ignoring Xander as he raised the arm holding the orb in his palm. "No walking away now, we're done talking. What say you?"

"I accept your offer," Michael said. "Goodbye, Eric."

"Goodbye, brother," Eric said then turned to Xander. "I hope you wake up before it's too late, Xan. Don't throw *your* life away."

Eric unleashed the orb.

It sped at Michael who shook his head slowly as the orb closed on his position. At the last possible second, he sidestepped the orb, allowing it to race past him. With a gesture, he released a tether of flaming energy which attached to the orb.

It kept racing past him for a few seconds, pulling the tether of flame tight. With a shift of his feet and a flick of his wrist, he redirected the orb back at Eric.

It raced back up the street too fast to track.

"You've made your choice," Eric said with a nod, outstretching his arms to his sides. "Thank you for making it fast."

Eric waited with his eyes closed.

Xander gestured and formed a large flame shield in front of Eric.

"That won't save him," Michael said. "It's too little, too late."

The orb shattered Xander's shield and crashed into Eric's body, disintegrating him where he stood.

"This was a waste of his life," Xander said, his voice angry and sad as he shook his head. "Goodbye, brother."

"He made his choice," Michael said. "We need to prep for the Inquisitor."

"You could have stunned him," Xander said as he whirled on Michael. "You had a choice."

"No, I didn't," Michael answered. "He chose the final rite. You saw his orb and you heard the choices—kill him, let him go, or die. What do you think would happen to us if we let him go? You know what would happen."

"We'd have Enforcers on us before the end of the day."

"Before the end of the hour!" Michael yelled. "You think I wanted to kill him? We couldn't just let him go, and I was not prepared to die today, were you? *Were you?*"

"No," Xander said. "I just think—"

"Stop thinking!" Michael said. "Thinking wasn't going to save Eric. Don't you see he was done? He chose his fate. I hate that he chose death, but *he* chose it, and I'm going to tell you right now, in case you might be confused.

"I'm not—"

"If I have to choose between seeing another dawn and accepting darkmages, I choose life—every time. Are we clear?"

"Absolutely," Xander said. "We'll need to report this."

"You draw it up and I'll authorize it," Michael said. "You'll have to affirm his actions as witness. Lethal force was the only outcome. He was gone."

Xander looked over to where Eric had stood.

"He didn't deserve this," he said. "Do we know which darkmage he spoke to?"

"Doesn't matter," Michael said. "Whoever it was got to

him and turned him. Damned darkmages. We need to wipe them all out."

"Is that really the solution?" Xander asked. "Hasn't seemed to work."

"Do you have another solution?" Michael asked, his voice calmer. "You have some insight that's greater than the Pentarch?"

"Of course not," Xander said. "It's just that darkmage genocide doesn't seem to be working. Do you think it's working?"

"Yes," Michael said. "Write the report, before Inquisitor Emery gets here."

ELEVEN

I placed a hand around my ring and poured as much power as I dared into it. They had just killed one of their own. If they discovered I was a darkmage, there would be no conversation, only an execution.

Mine.

My ring hummed with increased energy.

It should have reinforced my mask, hiding me from sight. I slowly made to leave the scene. I thought I would be able to leave undetected, but I heard the footsteps behind me.

Something was wrong.

"You there, stop where you are," Michael ordered, his voice stern. "We need a word."

This day had just taken a turn past bad and straight into horrific. They weren't supposed to be able to see me. Unless they were much stronger than they let on. I should have been a part of the background to their minds, something to be forgotten, but they saw me clearly.

The mask wasn't working at all.

"I'll handle this," Xander said, stepping in his path. "I cast the obscuring on her. I'll make sure it took effect."

"See that you do," Michael said, stopping his approach. "If not, she becomes a liability. One that needs to be eliminated."

"I understand," Xander said and began approaching me. "Excuse me, I need to speak to you."

Was it the obscuring cast that let them see through my mask? They should have forgotten about me. Why didn't they forget about me?

I could run.

I could move fast enough that he would be taken off-balance by my reaction. By the time he recovered, I would be a memory, fading into the shadows.

"Who me?" I asked innocently, remaining still before turning in his direction. "How can I help you?"

Xander stepped close to where I stood. Close enough for me to notice his chiseled jaw and rough good looks. I could tell he trained from the way his uniform fit his body.

I took a step back and he stopped where he stood.

His deep hazel eyes were filled with pain as he took a moment to compose himself. He looked behind him for a brief moment, where Eric had stood, before turning to face me again.

I lost myself in his gaze as he refocused on me. Eric was right. In these eyes, behind the mask of Enforcer, I could see more. Someone who cared, someone who felt pain at the loss of his brother. Someone tender.

Someone who just saw his Directorate brother cleansed because duty demanded it and let it happen. You can't trust him. He's dangerous. He's the enemy.

"What did you see?" he asked, placing a hand gently to my temple to scan my signature. "Did you notice anything out of the ordinary? Why were you on this street?"

"This is my usual route to and from the store," I said, looking around. "What was I supposed to see? This street looks the same as always."

"Pat's Deli?" he asked.

I nodded.

His hand was warm and pleasant on the side of my head as I focused on masking my signature. I really hoped my ring's power was strong enough. The routine scanning process resembled a gesture of concern. Placing a hand on the side of someone's head to determine their energy signature was usually a failsafe method, unless they were trained or had a powerful mask.

I kept my focus up, making sure to mask my true energy signature.

"That's good," he said as he focused his gaze on my face. "You seem to have some latent ability, nothing impressive. In another life, you could have joined the Directorate, maybe as a low-level clerk. Are you sure you didn't notice anything out of the ordinary?"

"Just a bunch of you arguing," I said, keeping my voice light as he removed his hand. "Then that other man left." I craned my neck around him. "Where did he go? He seemed like he was in a hurry."

I saw Michael behind him give a short nod of approval. He stared intently at me and stepped forward, handing me a card, which I accepted as I read.

Michael Holland, Directorate Enforcer, First Class, and a number beneath the name.

"He had another appointment to get to," Michael said, his voice somber as he looked around and glanced at Xander. "There are some dangerous individuals loose on these streets. If you see anything,"—he looked down at the card in my hand—"I want you to give me a call. My name is Enforcer Holland. Do you happen to live around here?"

If I lied, what was I doing down here alone? If I told him the truth, he might be back to check up on me at a later time. I needed to come up with a good excuse.

I was about to answer with a lie, when he turned away,

tapped a finger to his ear, and raised another finger in my direction, pausing my answer.

"One second, please," he said in my direction. "Yes, Holland here. Yes, we have one darkmage fugitive currently unaccounted for. No, the changeling doesn't matter. He'll be dead by nightfall. I hit him with a devourer. There won't be anything to find by dawn tomorrow. Only the darkmage matters now."

My stomach clenched at his words.

Xander pulled me to one side.

"Is someone hurt?" I asked. "Who will be dead?"

"Directorate business," he said, looking at me again and giving me a once-over. "Listen, you need to evacuate this area. It's going to be filled with...the authorities soon. If they find you here, they will want to hold you for questioning."

"Am I in trouble?" I asked. "I was just going to the store to get some milk—"

"Not at all," he said, his voice hitting all the right notes, making butterflies in the pit of my stomach flutter. "It's just a routine investigation. It doesn't concern you. Don't linger, you should go."

He is dangerous.

I nodded.

"Got it," I said, making to turn away. "Thank you for the warning."

"One more thing," he said, touching my arm and handing me his card. It was identical to the previous card except it read: *Xander Ashford, Directorate Enforcer*. There was no designation beneath his name just a number. "My associate is right—there are some dangerous individuals in this neighborhood. My name is Enforcer Ashford. If you do see anything out of the ordinary, please don't hesitate to contact me." He pointed to the card. "May I have your name for our records?"

"Val. Val Roqueforte," I said. "My friends call me V, but you can call me Val."

Clearly my brain had stopped functioning, and I had slipped into mindless ramble mode.

"Thank you, Miss Roqueforte," he said. "As I said earlier, it would be better if you weren't in the area when the Inquisitors arrive. They don't believe in innocent bystanders. To them, everyone is guilty until proven innocent."

I nodded again and walked away quickly, forcing myself not to look back. I used the reflection in the window across to the street to see him gesture and form a red teleport circle on the street under his feet.

A few seconds later, with a flash of deep red energy, he disappeared from sight.

Even after he was gone, I could still feel the dark and penetrating gaze.

He is the enemy. Stay away from him.

I picked up the milk and took an alternate route back to the house. Five blocks later, and while I was still a block away from the house, I felt a tug of power.

No. Not again.

I looked around quickly, but saw no mages.

This time it was different. This wasn't a surge of power. This was something deeper, primal and ancient. I kept following the feeling as it led me home.

I had crossed the threshold of the defenses around our property when the sense of power slammed into me, forcing the air from my lungs and nearly driving me to my knees. I leaned against a wall to keep my balance.

That's when I saw the body.

Lying unconscious on the ground, just inside the property was a young man. He looked to be in his early twenties and wore a variation of the Directorate uniform. His suit was black with gray accents. Along one sleeve, I could make out a series of symbols, but I didn't know what they meant. I knew he wasn't a mage, or if he was, I had never sensed a mage like him.

I gently turned him over on his back.

He looked normal in every respect except for his hair. It was mostly black, except for a large portion on one side of his head...which was a bright white.

For a brief moment, my heart seized.

Was he a darkmage? Was this the darkmage the Enforcers were looking for? Why would he come here, to my home? How did he get past the defenses?

As I crouched down near the body, Fen raced outside and met me.

"Who is that?" Fen asked, looking down at the body. "How did he get past the defenses?"

"I don't know," I said, seeing that the man was injured. "But he's hurt. Are we going to let him die in our yard?"

Fen scooped him up in his arms, and headed towards the house.

TWELVE

I noticed that the young man's suit had been torn across his chest. The right side of his chest was covered in a large, angry-looking, purple bruise. Around the bruise, the skin was discolored, and black lines of energy spiderwebbed across his side.

I noticed that the lines of energy were slowly expanding.

"Bleed me dry," Fen said under his breath as he shook his head. "He's dead."

"What do you mean he's dead?" I demanded. "It's clear he's breathing. Look at his chest. He's breathing!"

Fen looked down and focused on the bruise.

"You see that bruise? It's called a devourer. Nasty Directorate cast, favorite of the Enforcers. That bruise will expand. Once it gets a little deeper, it will start liquefying his organs."

"Liquefying?"

"That's why it's called a devourer," Fen said. "He must have run across an angry Enforcer. This cast is used to torture victims before killing them."

"We have to help him," I said. "We can't let him die."

"We aren't going to *let him* die," Fen said. "He's already dead. His body just hasn't gotten the message. He should have died by now. I've never seen a devourer get this large before."

"Can we stop it?" I asked. "He wants to live. That's why he's fighting it—he wants to live. We have to help him."

"I'm not a doctor," Fen said with a scowl. "Besides, I wouldn't know the first thing about stopping a devourer in its tracks. It's still expanding."

"Stopping it in its tracks?" I said as an idea came to me. "What is the base cast of a devourer? What discipline?"

"Forget it," Fen said, shaking his head. "You're not a doctor, either."

"I'm going to help him," I said, determined. "He's not going to die in our yard."

"No, you want him to die in our house," Fen said with a growl. "This is not a stray. He's wearing a Directorate uniform, it looks as if he was a low-level mage. I recognize most of those symbols, can you make out the rest?"

I shook my head.

"We can get a better look inside," I said. "Maybe one of the books in the library has those symbols?"

Fen shook his head, before looking around the property.

"This could be a trap," he said with a scowl. "He's not supposed to be able to get past our defenses. No one is. They should have fried him where he stood."

"Well, he's inside them and he's hurt," I said, making to touch the bruise before Fen shook his head. I looked into Fen's face. "We have to help him."

"I'll handle this," Fen said, effortlessly opening the front door as the young man stirred in Fen's arms. Fen looked down at him. "You have a name? Something I could put on your tombstone?"

"Melvichor," the young man said with a rasp. "Melvichor Ratel."

Then he promptly passed out.

"Melvichor," Fen said, mostly to himself as we entered the house. "Well, that's one hell of an entrance. You certainly took your time getting here."

Fen took him inside and placed him on the large table in the center of the living room. He gave me a glance and then looked at the door.

I nodded.

In our many years living together, we had developed an unspoken language. That look meant 'secure the door and activate the interior *and* exterior defenses'. I quickly moved to the door, pressed a panel near the entrance which caused the runes around the doorway to glow bright violet for a few seconds, before settling into a dull, barely visible purple.

Outside, all of the runic defenses on the property which had been passive, had switched to active. If anyone were to try and enter the property now, we would be sweeping up what was left of them.

Our defenses were lethal.

I made my way back to the table as Fen made Melvichor as comfortable as possible. While I was activating the defenses, he had gotten a black, rune-covered leather satchel. The runes were intricately etched into its surface, pulsing with a dormant power.

He placed the satchel on the table next to Melvichor.

"You know who he is?" I asked, looking at the young man's pale face. "What sort of name is Melvichor?"

"Old country," Fen said. "Haven't heard a name like that in ages. Not since my Guardian days."

"Do you know *who* he is?" I asked. "The way you said his name, it sounded like you knew him."

"I don't know who he is exactly," Fen began, then shook his head and held up a finger. "Wait, I *do* know who he is supposed to be, although I didn't expect him to show up with one foot inside death's door. What matters isn't who he is, but *what* he is."

"What he is?" I asked, looking down at the motionless Melvichor. "What is he? He looks like a regular person."

"Help me get the rest of his top off," Fen said, producing a blade as he proceeded to remove Melvichor's jacket and cut off what remained of his gray shirt. He handed me the clothing. "Take that and burn it, then scatter the ashes."

"Isn't that a bit much?" I said, giving him a look. "You act like his clothes are cursed or something."

"There's a good chance he has tracking runes on him somewhere," Fen said. "They should be disabled inside here, but let's not take any chances. Last thing we need are Enforcers knocking on our door."

"Burn them, though?"

"Do as I ask, please," he said. "Do you have anything foreign on your person?"

"Foreign?" I asked. "I went to get milk. Does that count?"

"And came back with him," Fen said, pointing at Melvichor. "Anything foreign? Anything that doesn't belong to you? Besides the milk and the nearly dead young man."

"No, nothing," I said, then remembered the cards the Enforcers gave me. "Nothing except these. Are these foreign?"

"Where did you get these?" he asked, examining them before placing the cards near the satchel. "These are Enforcer cards. There's a good chance they can trace them too."

"Really?"

He gave me a sharp nod and focused on Melvichor.

"I got them—"

I was about to continue when he raised a hand.

"Right now, if they do have tracking runes, they're

disabled because of our defenses," he said, looking down at Melvichor. "Let's see if we can save him. Then we deal with this."

He reached into the satchel and removed two thin black knives which held a blue tint, and placed them on the table. Silver runes ran the length of their blades as he examined the slowly growing bruise on Melvichor's chest.

"Can they help?" I asked, concerned. "Will they work?"

He grimaced as he looked at Mel.

"He has nothing to lose—except his life," Fen said, his face grim. "If the Needles don't work, we'll bury him out back, in the yard. While I do this part, debrief. What happened? There was a major surge not too far away. Were you involved in that?"

"Yes and no. What is he?" I asked again. "Tell me."

Fen had begun making small incisions around the devourer bruise with the two blades—the Needles. The runes on their blades made it possible for them to act as negators. If they managed to cut someone, they were able to undo casts and neutralize magic. One Needle was powerful, but if Fen used both, he was able to undo almost any cast, so long as blood was involved.

"Go get me some towels and water while I try and head off the spread of this bruise," he said, without looking up. When he sensed I hadn't moved, he let out a low growl. "Now. I'll tell you everything when you come back. Go. Hurry. The way this thing is spreading, he doesn't have longer than a few hours."

I ran off to the kitchen and grabbed some towels, along with a large pan and filled it with hot water. I made my way back to Fen without sloshing the water all over the place.

Blue-silver energy hovered over Melvichor's chest and Fen's hands as he held the Needles. He had nearly surrounded the entire bruise with semi-deep incisions. He had also used

Melvichor's blood to trace numbing runes on his body in an effort to aid in the pain management.

Fen wasn't really a doctor, but he knew enough to keep someone alive on a battlefield or at the very least, help them go with as little pain as possible if he couldn't save them.

"What can I do?" I asked. "Can I help?"

"Yes, if you can manage to control the flow," he said, still looking down at the cuts he was making. "I don't know if he's going to make it. We're going to do everything we can, but most of this depends on him. I'm surprised he's still alive, but I shouldn't be surprised really."

"What discipline is a devourer?" I asked. "What is the root?"

"Igneous," Fen said. "It takes root and then consumes. Do you understand how to approach this?"

"Aqua extinguishes Igneous," I said. "I've never dealt with Igneous this way."

"No time like the present," Fen said, glancing at me. "Remember stasis holds—"

"Stasis holds everything and nothing," I finished. "Stasis negates everything."

"You have to control the flow of your power," he said. "Release too much, and he dies in minutes as you stop everything inside of him—starting with his heart and lungs. Too little, and it does nothing, the devourer takes hold and ends him. You need to get the balance correct. If you do, we may save him."

"Thanks, no pressure," I said, taking a deep breath. "Can I touch the bruise? This will be easier if I can make contact."

"Touch the bruise, but don't touch the incisions I made," he said, his voice tight. "There's exposed energy there that is working to arrest the devourer. If you touch that with your power, it'll be like punching a hole in a dam. The devourer will do its best to get through the breach you create. Understand?"

"Got it," I said with a quick nod. "Touch the bruise, avoid the cuts."

"And control the flow."

"And control the flow," I repeated, stepping closer to Melvichor. "Find the right balance."

"Work from the center out," Fen said. "The Needles will act like a net, holding the devourer in check for now. If you work from the center out, you can trap the cast and destroy it. Find the root, undo it, and then work outward. Leave nothing."

"The point in the circle," I said, mostly to myself, remembering one of my early combat lessons. "Everything is combat."

"You are the point within the circle, and everything revolves around you," he said. "Right now, as you unleash your stasis, everything enters your orbit and you become the anchor. Can you see it?"

I nodded, but remained silent as I focused on Mel.

I saw him nod in my peripheral vision.

I took a few deep breaths and rested a hand on the bruise covering one side of Melvichor's chest. With my other hand, I gestured, allowing stasis energy to flow through my body.

The ring on my chest gave off a tone as if I had rung a bell.

Black energy converged around me, and even without seeing it, I knew my hair was turning white. I focused on the energy of the devourer, which felt like a large knot of power lodged in Melvichor's chest, similar to a tight muscle, only much harder.

I brought my other hand to rest next to the one touching the bruise and closed my eyes. Even with my eyes closed, I could see what I was doing.

I could feel the stasis energy flow through my body, down my arms and into my hands, and from there race into his chest. Melvichor spasmed and arched his back in response to the inflow of power.

Fen grabbed him and held him down.

"Easy," I heard Fen say, his voice distant. "Not so much, pull back a bit. Use a scalpel—"

"Not a machete," I finished as I reined in the flow of power. "Easier...said than done."

"Find the root of the devourer."

I let out a slow breath and let the stasis flow without filling the body below me. I was seeing the composition of the cast. Igneous casts were all chaos and energy, destroying what they interacted with. I let my power flow with the devourer energy until I found the still center of the cast—the root.

"Found it," I said, keeping my voice low. "It's buried deep."

"Means he has less time than I thought," Fen said. "Can you unravel it?"

"I don't know."

"If you don't do this, he dies," Fen said, an edge to his voice. "I've done everything I can. His life now rests in your hands."

I sent tendrils of my power into the root.

Initially there was a resistance, so I pushed, forcing more energy into Melvichor. The devourer reacted to my probing and resisted my approach.

"Easy," Fen said. "You can't brute force this. Finesse your way past the outer barrier."

I kept pushing gently.

The resistance held for a few seconds more, then gave way. I saw the actual root of the cast. It was a mass of energy that slowly expanded as it drew power from Melvichor's life force.

Igneous casts operated on a vicious self-perpetuating cycle.

The cast initially would attack a target and do damage, but the real danger and lethality came from the fact that it used the target's life force to continue powering the attack, creating a vicious loop of energy renewal that ended with the target dead and consumed.

"I'm past the outer barrier," I said, my voice strained. "This is trickier than I expected. I don't know if I can—"

"If you don't, we may as well wrap it up now," Fen said, cutting me off. "Either go all in, or stop now. Do not half-ass this."

"Anyone tell you your morale boosters need serious work?"

"My morale boosters do exactly what they need to do," he said. "What will it be?"

"We save him," I said. "He's not dying on my watch."

"Then get to the saving," he said. "Undo the root and obliterate everything that remains. Leave nothing of the cast or we will be right back here in a few days, trying to save his life. I don't have to tell you how much harder it will be if that happens."

"You don't," I said and unleashed more stasis. "He doesn't get a second chance with Igneous."

"He doesn't. Let's make this one count," Fen said as I felt the flow of his energy increase around the table. "The Needles are in place, it's all you now."

Fen had buried the Needles into the table around Melvichor, one near his head, the other near his feet. By doing this, he created a field of energy, a bubble around him that enhanced what I was trying to do.

Fen wasn't a mage, but he had some amazing abilities. What the Needles were doing was directly tied to his energy signature. He didn't manipulate energy like a mage, but he could control it through his blades.

"Thanks," I said, my voice tight. "I'm going to undo the devourer. We'll know soon enough if this works."

"You will make it work," Fen said, his voice leaving no room for doubt. "You can do this."

I wished I felt as confident as he sounded.

I unleashed the stasis energy and it raced out of me. For a brief moment, I almost lost control. It felt like taking hold of smoke as it slipped through my mental grasp. I took a breath and restored my grip on the energy.

"Stasis holds everything and nothing," Fen said under his breath. "Stasis negates everything."

I nodded as I withdrew the stasis into myself, refocused the energy and shot it into Melvichor. It blasted into his body, piercing the root and bisecting it. I shoved the stasis, and the energy shot out in every direction, cutting through the devourer and expanding to the outer limits of the cast.

With another mental shift, I transformed the stasis as I urged it into a vortex. As it began to rotate inside him, it started undoing the devourer.

This was a dangerous part of what I was trying to do. If I lost control, my stasis would destroy the devourer and keep undoing Melvichor, until nothing was left of him.

Not the result I was going for.

This is what Fen meant about maintaining the balance of the flow. I had to let the stasis undo the devourer, but keep enough control that it didn't harm or kill Melvichor.

Sweat was pouring into my eyes as I maintained control.

This was more than I had ever attempted with my stasis. If it had manifested fully, this whole procedure would have been easy—well, easier. Since my power was still mostly dormant, it was like trying to hold flowing water with my hands—nearly impossible.

Fen ran a towel across my forehead, which I appreciated.

There was one final step, which was the most dangerous.

Without my power fully manifested, I would have to use my ring as the anchor. I would tap into it and unleash the reservoir of energy it contained. It would boost the energy that was currently flowing and hopefully destroy what remained of the devourer.

Or it could completely undo Melvichor.

THIRTEEN

I had never done something this complicated, so there was a good chance this could all go horribly wrong.

"Last...part," I said, opening my eyes and placing one hand around the ring around my neck. "If this goes wrong..."

"It won't," Fen said, squeezing my shoulder. "You have this. Remember who you are, what you are. You are a darkmage, and what do darkmages do?"

"Darkmages overcome and conquer."

"Always," he said.

"Still," I said, catching my breath before I reached for the power in the ring. "You may not want to be at ground zero if this goes darkmage disaster on me."

"That's not a real thing and it won't," Fen said. "Finish it and save him."

I took a deep breath, closed my eyes again, and let it out with a nod.

I whispered a word of power.

Undula.

It was one of the few I knew in darkmage. The closest

definition of the word was *to oscillate*, to create a back and forth interaction with energy.

My ring thrummed again with a lower tone and the energy flowed out of it. I could feel it hovering all around me before it swirled around my body and shot into my chest, boosting my own internal energy and increasing the flow into Melvichor.

This is what it would feel like when I fully manifested my energy, except the power, the stasis I controlled would be all mine, not borrowed from the ring.

My mental process sharpened and I took hold of the energy with a quick thought. The stream of energy narrowed as the intensity increased. With my darksight fully engaged, I was able to direct the stasis.

I directed it to undo all of the devourer cast and then attempted to shut it down. Everything had worked—the devourer was gone with no trace left in Melvichor's body.

There was only one problem: the stasis was still increasing.

"I can't stop it," I said, panicked as my hand was now connected to Melvichor. It was as if I had taken a live electrical current into my hand. I couldn't pull away. I looked on in horror as the stasis, a black cloud of charged energy, began to grow around me and Melvichor. "It's getting out of control."

Fen looked around and reached for one of the Needles. Before he could grab it, Melvichor's eyes shot open and he moved. He grasped my ring and whispered some words I couldn't understand.

The black energy swirling around us froze in place and I stood in a thick cloud of stasis energy. Melvichor looked into my eyes, and I could feel a tether of energy form between us. His eyes flashed with blue-black stasis energy as the ring reversed the flow of power.

A lightning crack of blue energy landed between us. It blinded me, unleashing a blast of energy that flung me and Fen across the living room with force. I bounced off the wall and landed hard. Fen recovered with more grace, rolling to one side and ending up on his feet. I was trying to get my bearings when a bass rumble of thunder, which resembled a freight train crashing through the house, shattered the silence of the room.

Melvichor looked at where I lay and locked eyes with me. I saw another blue-black flash in his eyes as I met his gaze.

"Thank you," he said. "My bonded."

Then he promptly passed out.

"What was that?" Fen asked when he found me sprawled behind one of the smaller tables. "What did you do?"

"I did what I was supposed to do," I said, gathering myself, but still unclear as to what it was I'd done. "You wanted me to save him, we saved him...I think. Did it work?"

"I said save him, not try to destroy the house with a blast of darkmage energy," Fen said as he moved over to where Mel lay and checked him. He removed the Needles and wiped them down with a dry towel, placing them back in the satchel as he shook his head in amazement. "What kind of cast was that?"

"Which part?" I answered, still dazed. My brain was having some trouble getting back up to speed on what had just happened. "How is he?"

"I don't know what you did—" he started and pointed at Mel.

"*I* don't know what I did," I said. "Did we save him?"

"The devourer is gone," Fen said, still looking at the unconscious Mel. "How did you do that? With the lightning?"

"What part of 'I don't know what I did' is unclear?" I said, annoyed. More at myself than at Fen, because I felt I should have known what happened. My annoyance was really fear at nearly losing control and nearly obliterating not only Mel, but Fen and myself too. The not knowing scared me deeper than I was willing to admit. "I don't know. As soon as I do, you will too."

He nodded and made to move Mel from the table.

"I'm just going to move him to—"

"Hold on," I said, holding up a hand and unsteadily getting to my feet. "He said something there, before he passed out."

"Caught that, did you?"

"Apparently so did you," I said, giving him my 'don't BS me' glare. "What did he mean 'my bonded'?"

"That was the other part of what I was going to tell you," Fen said. "This is Melvichor, your other Guardian, and also...a changeling."

"My other what?" I said, raising my voice. "He's a what? Come again?"

"He's your other Guardian and also a changeling," Fen said, taking Mel into his arms. "Let me move him off this table. When I get back, I'll answer all your questions. Try not to blow up the house in the meantime."

"Wait," I said before he left the living room. "Something happened before the blast. Something happened between us."

"You mean the part where you nearly blew apart our home?"

"Before that," I said, touching Mel's forehead. "The stasis flowed between us."

"Between you?" Fen asked, looking down at Mel. "He's not a darkmage. I mean, granted the hair is unique, but it's not like yours." He sniffed the air around Mel. "He's distinctly *not* a darkmage. Speaking of"—he turned to leave the room—"fix your hair and your face."

"Fix my—?"

"I'm all for makeovers, except *that* one can get you killed," he said. "Be right back."

He nodded in my direction, looking at the top of my head before nodding over to the large mirror on the other side of the living room.

I moved over to the large mirror as he left the room and stood in stunned silence. Not only had all of the hair on my head turned a bright white, but my eyebrows and eyelashes had joined in on the bright white party.

My eyes, which were normally a dark brown, almost black, had a distinct violet tinge to them.

"If this doesn't scream darkmage, I don't know what does." I took a deep breath and let it out as I focused. "I really need a more permanent solution. Maybe there's some sort of runic dye that could work on me."

"Doubtful," Fen said as he re-entered the room. "I spent a small fortune and tried every dye in existence when you were younger. None withstood your stasis outbursts. Not for long, at least."

"Not one?"

"None," he said with shake of his head. "Not even partially."

I crossed my arms and glared at him.

"You have questions, I'm sure," he continued. "Ask."

"You let me unleash my stasis on him," I said, upset. "I could've killed him."

"Not a question."

"Why did you let me unleash my stasis, especially when it hasn't fully manifested?"

"He would be dead if you hadn't," he said. "You know I'm right."

"Being right doesn't matter."

"Ah, but *you* know I'm right," he said. "Matters to me."

"Who is he?" I asked. "I already know he's a changeling. Thanks for that bit of information before I unleashed a potentially body-altering cast on an unsuspecting victim."

"His name is Melvichor Ratel."

"I got that part from him," I said. "Tell me the other details."

"When you first arrived with the Traveler, his name was mentioned," Fen said. "Do you recall?"

"I was a child," I said. "And all I really remember from that day was how scary you were."

"True, but you weren't like most children," he said, removing a card from a pocket. "I've been keeping this for you since that day."

He handed me the card.

"What's this?" I said, looking at the embossed black card. It had a name and an address. No phone number and no other details. "Who is Moira Redmond? What's at 1 Catherine Lane?"

"The Traveler gave me that for you," he said. "I tried to get information on her over the years; it was beyond scarce. Went by the address a few times. It's not even a proper street. There's nothing on it—a few doors, but nothing else. Was thinking of asking Wheels—he is connected enough to have a lead of some kind."

"This Moira is a darkmage?"

"I don't know," Fen said. "But if she is, that address looks like a front. There's a good chance she will be at the Tombs."

"The Tombs?" I said remembering a trip we took underground long ago. He had business with some darkmages in an area beneath the subway system of the city. "That place was creepy."

"By design," he said. "The Directorate avoids the place."

"Why?"

"It's bad for their health," he said. "The mages they send

down there to investigate usually end up with a terminal case of perforation."

"Do you know who's eliminating them?"

"No, and I never thought to investigate," he answered. "I may be many things, but suicidal isn't one of them."

"Why are you giving me this now?"

"My gut tells me you're going to need that soon," Fen said. "This Moira is supposed to teach you when your powers manifest."

"My powers haven't—" I started.

He looked around the destruction in the living room, and I followed his gaze with my own.

"What you did with the changeling says different," he said. "You're more than ready. However, this might change our plans a bit."

"Change our plans?"

"That blast," he said, looking up. "If the Directorate didn't notice that, then they must be blind and deaf. That much power will get attention, plenty of it. Only a matter of time before they pinpoint the location. You'll have to find another way to infiltrate the Directorate."

"Not if I can't get this transformation under control."

"Why do mages die?"

"They become complacent," I said. "They miss the details and become fatally lax."

"What *must* you exploit?"

"Overestimation and underestimation," I said. "Present weakness when I'm strong, and strength when I'm weak."

"Exactly," he said, pointing to my hair. "Restore the camouflage."

"*Furvus,*" I muttered to myself in darkmage as I let power flow into my head, turning the white hair back to jet black. "Better?"

"Much," he said as he fixed the furniture in the living

room. "That changeling was looking for you. Which means Directorate Enforcers will be looking for him."

"They were after him and a darkmage. I didn't see the darkmage, though; I don't think they were together," I said and pointed to where Mel rested. "They dismissed him for dead."

"They hit him with a devourer," Fen said, picking up the cards the Enforcers had given me. "By all rights, he should be dead."

"They were focused on the darkmage," I said, thinking back to Enforcer Holland's words. "An Inquisitor was getting involved."

"An Inquisitor?" Fen asked, suddenly alert. "Are you sure?"

"Yes, they both made references to reinforcements and an Inquisitor."

"Enforcers Holland and Ashford," he said, looking at the cards. "Which one hit him with the devourer?"

"Holland," I said. "He also cleansed a fellow Enforcer, Eric, for defying him."

His expression darkened.

"I see. What about this Ashford?" Fen asked. "What did you sense about him?"

"He's a Directorate Enforcer," I said, my words hard. "I consider him an enemy."

"As you should."

"But..."

"But?"

"He's conflicted," I said. "Holland is clear about his purpose. He exists to carry out the will of the Pentarch. He lives for the Directorate. Ashford...I think he can be turned, or at the very least convinced he's on the wrong path. There's hope for him. Slim, but it's there."

Fen nodded.

"I know you have questions, but we need to go over what

happened. Now," Fen said, looking at the cards he held and then at the door. "We're running out of time."

"We're running out of time?"

"Memorize the information and destroy them," he said, holding out the cards to me. "Do it. Now."

FOURTEEN

I scanned the cards, memorizing the information, then let a trickle of stasis energy flow. It hit the cards and disintegrated them, turning them to dust.

Fen shook his hands of the dust and motioned for me to follow him. We headed down to the garage, where he unlocked one of the weapons safes by placing a hand on the wall panel next to it.

He opened the door and I saw the assortment of blades and guns. He removed several thigh sheathes and a snug holster—one of my favorites which I used when he let me wear Stinger, my gun.

He opened Gladys' trunk and placed several bags inside.

"What are you doing?" I asked, confused. "Where are we going?"

"*We* aren't going anywhere," he said. "Debrief. Make it short and sweet."

I explained the interaction I witnessed between the Directorate Enforcers.

"Bleed me dry," he said under his breath. "This happened on the street? Were there other people around?"

"No," I said, shaking my head. "They used something to clear out the streets—"

"Aversion runes," he said. "Streets were deserted. They must have cast them after you accidentally entered their cordon. Do you know who cast the aversion runes?"

"Holland," I said. "I heard Ashford refer to them not holding up indefinitely. These were the regular patrol Enforcers."

"They don't," Fen said. "Aversion runes are for short jobs. Enforcers prefer them for shock and awe operations."

"How do you know?"

"Enforcer SOP," he said. "How soon before they saw you?"

"Took a while," I said. "My mask was working."

"Until it wasn't," he said. "Aversion runes can sometimes scramble masks. Nasty side effect."

I nodded.

"Ashford saw me first, though I'm pretty sure all of them did."

"What discipline were they?"

"All of them were Igneous."

"Makes sense," Fen said, mostly to himself. "Enforcers and all. Did you deviate from your usual route?"

"No," I said, offended. "I took the route I always take. I took my usual precautions; they weren't looking for me, and I was masked."

"That you know of."

"They had a duel in the street," I countered. "It wasn't like I was looking for them. They were focused on the changeling and a darkmage."

He raised an eyebrow at me.

"A different darkmage, not me," I clarified. "Besides they were too busy facing off against each other to focus on old, *normal* me."

"In broad daylight?" Fen asked, then caught himself. "Of course in broad daylight, what am I saying? Any collats?"

"No, none," I said. "The street was empty."

"The lack of collateral damage means this Holland person was stronger than the usual Enforcer," Fen said. "This is not good. Tell me they didn't scan you."

"I can tell you that, but it won't be the truth."

His expression darkened.

"Who scanned you?"

"Ashford."

"Why did he scan you?"

"He released an obscuring cast and a memory cloud on me," I said. "It didn't work, because of the ring."

"Your next answer is going to be very important," Fen said with a level of intensity in his voice I rarely heard. "I want you to think carefully before you answer, understand?"

I nodded my head, concerned at the tone in his voice.

"I understand, ask."

"At any point in this interaction did your focus slip?"

"No. Not even for a second."

"How did he see you if you were masked?"

"I...I don't know," I said, unsure. "But I was masked completely. He didn't know who or what I was, even after the physical scan. Was it possible the scan interfered with the mask?"

"Improbable, but not impossible."

"Well, it didn't work."

"That much is clear or we wouldn't be having this conversation," he said as he moved to the large closet in the rear of the space. "He would've placed you in custody, and I would've been fighting the Directorate to break you out at this very moment."

"Or sweeping up my ashes," I said, thinking back to Eric's

death. "Holland didn't seem big on apprehending anyone. He was acting like judge, jury, and executioner."

"Did Ashford share his zeal for death?"

"No," I said. "He wanted to take it back to Directorate HQ. He tried to resolve it without violence."

"That's a rare Enforcer. Are you certain you cleared the physical scan?" he asked. "You gave nothing away?"

"I thought he was attractive," I said. "But I didn't tell him that. He had the most amazing eyes."

Fen raised an eyebrow and stared at me for a few seconds.

"Earth to Val," he said, snapping his fingers. "What did he say? Exactly? Did he say more after you were lost in his amazing eyes?"

"Yes, he was even concerned for my safety," I said. "Told me I needed to get to safety, that I needed—"

"To get off the streets before the authorities flooded the scene?"

"Yes," I said, confused. "How did you know?"

"Think carefully. Was this statement followed by a red teleport circle and then he vanished from sight?"

"How do you know that?" I asked, worried. "That's exactly what happened."

He tossed me a large bag while grabbing another and tossing it into Gladys.

"Again, SOP," he said. "Tell me you made sure you weren't followed."

"Of course I wasn't followed," I snapped. "I didn't lose my mind over a pair of eyes, no matter how amazing they looked. He watched as Holland killed his Enforcer brother for defying the Directorate. As far as I'm concerned, he helped kill him."

"This Eric defied the Directorate? How?" Fen asked, curious. "Did they say what it was? Enforcers don't attack each other unless one of them violates the Directorate edicts."

"Over darkmages."

"What?" Fen said, shooting me a sharp glance. "Explain."

I explained some of the things Eric had been saying to Holland.

"Shit, this is bad," Fen said. "The most logical conclusion will be that this Eric was in the area to see some darkmage who was filling his head with darkmage concepts. It would be considered sacrilege to the Directorate—especially the Enforcers. They must have intercepted him."

"Enforcer Holland killed him," I said, my voice hard. "His own Enforcer brother. He disintegrated him."

"Imagine what he will do to you if he finds you," he said, adjusting another bag over the first. "Anything else you need?"

"No, you taught me to travel light," I said, angry. Mostly at myself for falling for the obvious ploy. "How long do we have?"

"This Ashford scanned you," Fen said, moving to a control panel near the rear entrance. "The defenses on the property bought us some time. They will make it difficult to locate you. You aren't the problem; I think the changeling may have been tracked too. If that's the case, we have fifteen on the outside. Less, if he's very, very good."

"He's better than he let on."

"He must have seen through your responses," Fen said, his voice tight as he shook his head. "It's possible you were dazzled by the way the light hit his eyes."

"I acted like a rank amateur; how could I be so *stupid?*" I said. "I should have never let him scan me."

"No, not stupid, never stupid." He pointed a finger at me. "Careless perhaps, but not stupid," he said and paused, turning to the panel. "Scrub protocol, Fenrir."

"Scrub protocol initiated," said an electronic female voice from the panel. "Thirty minutes to implementation of scrub protocol completion. Please exit the premises."

Scrub protocol was a cast Fen used that would remove all organic traces from a specific location. No fingerprints, no DNA, nothing that could trace back to us.

It was quick, efficient and deadly.

We had to be gone before the scrub protocol started.

Or we would be part of the organic material the protocol destroyed.

"You need to go, now," Fen said, closing the panel. "This place is burned for at least a year."

"What do you mean?" I asked. "You're coming with me, right?"

"Right now, I'm going to get Melivichor," he said. "Then, I'm going to buy you some time."

"Buy me some time?" I asked, still confused. "But we'll meet up at a safe house, right?"

"Of course," he said and headed upstairs. "Go get anything you think you might need and then get Gladys outside. Keep her engine running."

"You're letting me drive her?"

"The way I taught you, yes," he said. "Get ready."

"Damn it," I said. "I'm sorry, Fen."

"Don't be sorry, be moving," he said, his expression serious. "We need to get your ass out the door. You need to ghost this place before your Enforcer with the beautiful eyes shows up."

"That's not funny," I said. "Do I need to remind you of Lila?"

"Ouch," Fen said with a wince. "No need to be cruel. Move."

He ran down the corridor and headed upstairs to get Melvichor.

I got into Gladys and started her engine.

The roar of the engine brought a reflexive smile to my face. Gladys was a matte black, '67 Shelby Mustang GT500.

I heard the explosion as I rolled outside.

"What the hell—?" I said, turning my head around.

Fen came into my rear-view mirror with Mel next to him; both were moving fast. Mel got into the passenger seat and gave me a tight smile.

"No need for a scrub protocol now," Fen said under his breath. "Seems they really wanted to have a word with you."

"Yes, just one—goodbye."

Fen nodded.

"Gladys will get you out of here," Fen said, tapping the hood. "Won't you, girl? She'll take good care of you."

"Wouldn't it be easier for us to teleport out of here?"

"And leave Gladys behind? Blasphemy," he said. "Besides, I can guarantee you that whoever blew up the house above us has mage trackers in their group. They'll follow a teleport and wait for us where we show up. No, thanks."

He reached into the safe and put on an assortment of weapons, the last being an array of blades on each leg in custom sheaths. He handed me my holster, Stinger, and the thin black satchel holding Needles.

"Those are yours," I said, looking at him. "What are you—?"

"They're yours now," he said. "You know how to use them. You have plenty of ammo for Stinger in the trunk. When you run out, you know who to see."

I nodded, forcing myself not to cry.

"Don't you dare," he said. "This isn't goodbye. This is until later."

"Which safe house are we meeting at?" I asked, holding on to the lie. "Do you know?"

"Right now, I want you to stay off-grid," he said, making sure his guns were loaded. "Head to that address I gave you, put Gladys in storage with Wheels—you know where—once it's safe to do so. Once I've lost the Directorate, I'll reach out to you."

Another lie.

"Off-grid?" I asked. "What does that even mean? They probably have all sorts of vehicles designed to stop us."

"This here is a '67 Shelby Mustang GT500, designed to outrun and own anything on the road," Fen said lovingly, patting the hood again. "She will not be left behind nor abandoned. She'll take good care of you." He turned to the dash. "You'll show them, won't you, Gladys?"

I smiled at the speech I had heard more times than I could remember. The roar of the engine filled the garage as I stepped on the accelerator.

He squeezed my shoulder and rubbed my head.

"You need to get going, now," he said and looked past me at Mel. "Make sure you keep her safe. As if your life depended on it."

Mel nodded.

"I will," Mel said. "I won't let you down."

"See that you don't," Fen said, tapping the hood one last time before heading back into the house. I could hear raised voices upstairs. "Use the bug-out protocol, Kitsune. Now get your ass out of here."

Another series of low explosions rocked the top floors.

"This would be a good time to exit the premises, don't you think?" Mel said. "Unless you want to stay and tear them all apart. Whatever you decide, I will be by your side."

"I want to tear them apart, but we can't stay. I, we, still have too much to do," I said, struggling with every word. The pit of my stomach twisted into a knot as I stepped on the accelerator again. When the roar of the engine died down, I looked upstairs where the sound of gunfire had erupted. "Goodbye, Fen."

We raced away from the garage, much to the surprise of the Directorate vehicles stationed on the corner. I doubted they expected anyone beating a hasty retreat after those explosions, much less in a black muscle car designed for speed.

FIFTEEN

In the middle of the morning, Gladys was a shadow of speed, racing away from the garage and down the street. Being three blocks away from the Westside Highway wasn't a coincidence. Fen always picked out places close to main thoroughfares to allow us a quick escape if needed.

In the brief seconds before we sped down the block, I saw the Directorate vehicles. I counted at least three Tormentors and one containment van. Whoever had activated this squad thought we were a threat—maybe not much of one, but enough to warrant the Tormentors.

"Three Tormentors is a little light," I said as we sped down the street. "I'm almost offended."

"I don't think they realize who you *really* are," Mel said as I swerved around traffic on the Westside Highway. "If they knew they were pursuing Alfonse Forza's granddaughter, we'd have a fleet of at least twenty Tormentors with significant air support on our tail, along with the full might of the Directorate unleashed upon us."

I shot him a glance.

"What did you say?" I asked. "How did you—?"

"I know who you are," he said. "We're bonded. That means no secrets between us."

"Who gave you that information?" I said, shocked and surprised at how matter-of-factly he mentioned who I was. Who I *truly* was. "Who have you spoken to?"

"You know me as I know you," he said. "It's part of the bond."

"Somehow my brain didn't get that memo," I shot back. "All I know is your name and that you're a changeling."

"Your power has started to manifest. Once it grows to full strength, our bond will deepen, revealing more. As you grow more powerful, so will I."

"Who told you about my grandfather?"

"*You* told me," he said calmly. "When you removed the devourer from my body. That blast wasn't me, that was *you*. I was merely the key, you opened the door—well, more like kicked the door open."

"That blast was me?" I said in disbelief as I raced up the Westside Highway. "That's impossible."

"I think, right now," he said as he turned to look behind us, "we have bigger problems, don't you?"

He pointed to the group of vehicles behind us.

"Damn it," I hissed. "This isn't over. You have a lot of explaining to do."

We had gotten some distance away when I heard another, louder explosion. I looked in the rear-view mirror and knew what had happened. The area where my home, our home sat, was billowing smoke.

"Fen..." I said.

"He never planned to meet you at a safe house," Mel said, looking out of the passenger window. "You know this. He is the reason there are only three and not ten or more Tormentors behind us. He bought us time and a chance."

"He could have survived that," I said, hoping against hope. "Fen is nearly impossible to kill."

"I truly hope he did," Mel said, still looking out of the window. "He seemed formidable. If he didn't survive, I will make sure to avenge his death. The Directorate will pay for this day with their blood."

He was sounding a little dark, but I figured he had gone through a near-death experience recently and was entitled to a certain amount of latitude in the feeling vengeful department.

"How did they even find us?" I asked myself as I cut off some traffic and tried to put vehicles between us and our Directorate pursuers. "I was careful. I was more than careful, but Fen said—"

"One of the Enforcers scanned you," Mel said. "I saw him when he did. That was the catalyst."

"How did you—?"

"I have excellent camouflage," he said. "I couldn't assist you; I had the devourer in me at that moment and was in the process of preventing my death."

"The scan? I was masked," I said. "There was no way."

"The scan was only part of it," he said as I accelerated past some insane taxicabs. "It was mostly my and Deanna's fault."

"Deanna? Who is Deanna?"

"The darkmage who escaped with me," he said. "I don't know if she made it."

"You two were together?"

"No, she helped me get past the Enforcers."

"But you were wearing an Enforcer uniform, or something close to it."

He looked down at his new clothing. Fen had provided him with combat armor similar to mine after we had shredded and burned his previous set of clothing.

He didn't carry any weapons, at least none I could see. Maybe changelings possessed internal weapons? There were more questions than answers with my new Guardian.

"I was being held against my will," he said. "Used for infiltration operations. They had me join darkmage cells and then report the location of the cell to the Enforcers tasked with its elimination."

"Let me guess," I said, "You were recently reporting to Michael and Xander."

He nodded.

"Among others, but Michael was the lead Enforcer on my current operation," he answered. "When I reported the most recent location, Michael deemed me a liability. Said I had been corrupted by the darkmages. He was going to kill me, but Deanna intervened."

"But he hit you with a devourer."

"Partially," Mel said, his voice serious. "He had hit, and killed, several darkmages before he targeted me. Deanna caused him to miss by confronting him. I lost her in the chaos that ensued, and I'm sure he's livid at the thought of her getting away."

"He thinks you're dead."

"I should be after that devourer," he said. "You saved me. I couldn't hold on much longer. I owe you my life—thank you."

"They forced you to work for them?" I asked. "That's how he had your signature?"

He nodded.

"The blast that signaled our bond will read like a stasis blast," he replied, glancing at me. "They won't have your signature, but you can't let an Inquisitor scan you...ever. You won't be able to hide from one of their scans. They're too strong."

"I don't plan on meeting an Inquisitor...ever."

"You will, you have to...eventually," he said. "What you're looking for is *inside* the Directorate HQ."

"How do you know what I'm—"

"The Eclipse," he said. "You need it and you're going to need help in getting it."

"How do you know about—? Nevermind, we'll get to that later. Your signature gave us away? How?"

"This is just my theory; I'm not a mage, so I may be wrong," Mel said. "Michael had my energy signature through the devourer. Once we bonded, that blast broadcast my location, allowing him to locate me."

"Even through our defenses?"

"Yes, even through the defenses at your home," he said. "You could say they found us because *we* told them where we were."

"You theory sounds thin," I said. "My mask—"

"Wasn't enough after we bonded," he said. "You need to learn how to control your abilities better. You need a stronger mask now."

"Michael ordered a property cleansing for one changeling?" I said, incredulous, as I weaved through traffic. We were going to run out of road eventually. "Isn't that overkill? He made it seem like he didn't care about you."

"If I was dead," Mel said. "The blast proved I wasn't. Which means I am a loose end. He isn't one to leave loose ends dangling. My being alive would make him look irresponsible and incompetent, something his ego will not allow him to tolerate."

"By eliminating you, he's covering his tracks."

Mel nodded.

"The Directorate is taking measures," Mel said. "cracking down on any aberrations they find."

"I am not an aberration," I said. "Neither are you. We have a right to live just like they do."

"I don't think they agree," Mel said. "Michael blasted me with the devourer before I had a chance to react. I was caught off-guard. You have no idea how difficult it is to do that to a changeling—he is dangerous."

"Could they be just after you?" I asked. "Can they still track you?"

"It's likely," he said. "I would need to change form to throw them completely off my energy signature, but I'm still too weak from the devourer."

"So, they think you made it to our house?" I asked. "Hid out there and then what, met up with a darkmage, who proceeded to blast a signal to alert them of your location?"

"I doubt they are pursuing a darkmage signature," he said. "Right now, I'm fairly certain they are only tracking me. Until I can change, Michael will have my location, which he can impart to the Enforcers pursuing us."

"You don't think he's back there?"

"With only three Enforcers? No," Mel said. "I'm sure there are Enforcers behind us, but it won't be Michael. I'm not important enough to warrant his presence. He will delegate my capture to a lower Enforcer."

"Someone he can blame, if we manage to escape."

"Yes, he will need a scapegoat."

"Xander?"

"Unlikely," Mel said. "He is nearly a First Class Enforcer. He would send a Third Class after a weakened changeling, perhaps a Second Class, but not Xander."

"How long until you're strong enough to change?"

"I need at least another ten to fifteen minutes," he said. "Can you stall them that long?"

"How certain are you that they're only after a changeling?"

"You mean as opposed to you?"

"Yes."

"We wouldn't be facing only three Tormentors if they

were after you," he said. "We'd be facing the Echelon One Directorate Task Force if they thought they were pursuing Forza's granddaughter."

"True," I said, angry. "The blast must have alerted them to you. I'm sorry."

"No time to worry about that now," he said as he looked in the rear-view mirror. "Heads up. We have company. Do you think you can lose them?"

The three Tormentors were closing in on our position. Tormentors were black vehicles that were a hybrid between an armored truck and a large SUV. They were distinct and particular to the Directorate. Once you saw one, you never confused them for any other type of vehicle.

The Directorate emblem of the large red crown with the sword through it also helped with recognition. No other vehicle would dare use that emblem and try to imitate the Directorate. Tormentors struck fear in the heart of every mage who had the bad luck to run across one.

Lucky me, I had three chasing us.

I opened the window.

The blast of air hit me in the face as I leaned out of Gladys. I needed a good angle to be able to hit the lead Tormentor.

"Do you know how to drive?" I asked, glancing at Mel. Fen would kill me if he knew what I was planning next. "Can you hold her steady?"

"What are you doing?" Mel asked, surprised, as I slid out of the window. "I do, but I don't think this counts as driving."

"Keep your eyes on the road and just hold her steady," I said, keeping my foot on the gas pedal. "I'm going to slow them down a bit."

"Valentina, you can't," he warned. "If you use your dark-mage ability, even diminished as it is, they will know they're in pursuit of a darkmage. They will contact the Directorate and it won't just be three Tormentors after us, we'll have the *entire* Directorate after us."

"First of all, it's Val or Kit," I said, a pang of pain gripping me as I said my nickname. "No one calls me Valentina. Second"—I formed an orb of ice—"I'm a fairly decent ice mage. I guess the bond didn't give you *that* information?"

He looked on, surprised at the dark blue orb that formed in my hand.

"How—?" he started. "That's ice, not stasis?"

I nodded as I released the orb I had formed and watched as it raced at the lead Tormentor. It slammed into the windshield and instantly covered it with a thick layer of ice.

I nodded with satisfaction as I turned and sat back in the driver's seat and took hold of the wheel.

"Got him," I said and pumped a fist. "One Tormentor down, two to go."

"Don't celebrate just yet," Mel said. "Look again."

A blaze of flame had covered the windshield, melting my ice in seconds. They had barely slowed down in the time it took to melt my orb attack.

"They have Enforcers in that Tormentor," I said. "If I use my ability, it would stop all three of them at once."

"And alert the Directorate to the location of a powerful darkmage," Mel said, shaking his head. "Namely, you. Perhaps, instead of hitting the windshield, try the road. It should cause them to swerve off the highway."

"That may cause collats," I said, shaking my head. "I'm not trying to kill innocent drivers out here."

"If you freeze the road just in front of them, they won't have time to react," he said. "They will either have to stop or slide into the ice and crash. There's no other traffic around us at the moment; there won't be any collateral damage. Hit the road and then get off the Highway in a hurry."

Was Xander in one of those Tormentors? Was he cruel enough to attempt to kill us based on Michael's orders or incomplete information? There was no way he could have scanned me properly. He barely touched me.

"Hello?" Mel said, raising his voice. "This would be a good time to release that orb!"

His voice shook me out of my thoughts as I let go of the orb. It raced at the lead Tormentor that was waiting for another attack. I saw the windshield begin to glow red as the orb closed on it. At the last second, the orb dropped to the road, freezing a large patch of the Westside Highway.

Like Mel said, they didn't have time to react. The lead Tormentor hit the brakes and skidded right onto the ice patch that had formed. It slid to the side and slammed into the Tormentor on the left, which crashed into the concrete divider and then rebounded back into the lead Tormentor.

This caused a domino effect which shoved the lead truck into the Tormentor on the right. In seconds, they had all skidded to a stop as their engines smoked.

I stepped on the gas, increasing the distance between us. with a quick backward glance I saw the containment van pull up to the three vehicles and breathed a sigh of relief as I leaned back in my seat.

SIXTEEN

"At least we stopped them," I said, maintaining our speed. "That Enforcer in the lead car didn't know when to quit."

"He still doesn't," Mel said. "Determined Enforcer on our six, coming in fast."

I turned suddenly to look behind us.

In the distance, I noticed there was a motorcycle approaching.

On it, I briefly caught the red and black colors of an Enforcer. His face was covered by a helmet, which meant I couldn't make out the details of who was following us—even his energy signature felt strange, but I knew everything I needed to know.

He was an Enforcer, and he wasn't going to stop until he caught us...or died in the process. I wasn't going to let him catch us, which only left one option.

"I may have to unleash the power now," I said, determined. "If he gets any closer, he can slag Gladys. I can't let him apprehend us."

"Unleashing your stasis power is not a wise course of action," Mel warned. "He's more vulnerable on that motorcycle than in the Tormentor. How about a targeted snow storm, just for our new Enforcer friend? Can you pull *that* off as an ice mage?"

"I can," I said, giving the idea some thought. "It wouldn't be as permanent as hitting him with a stasis null blast, but fine."

"You're trying *not* to attract the rest of the Directorate," Mel said. "Right now, you're just a rogue ice mage, a minor inconvenience to be dealt with and dispatched. Let's not give him any reason to think differently."

"Just so you know, this is a short-term solution," I said. "It's only going to delay him for a short time, ten to fifteen minutes, max."

"We can use that window of inactivity to disappear."

"That's not a very long time."

"I'm aware. Anytime you're ready. I think now would be good," Mel said, nervous, as the roar of the motorcycle's engine grew closer. "He's closing on us."

I gestured and then extended my hand out of the driver's side window as I accelerated Gladys. Blue energy formed around my hand and spread out next to the car. My exhalation was a thick cloud as the air behind us became super cooled.

In moments, the ambient moisture in the air around us began to freeze, causing a large stream of snow to form behind us, creating blizzard conditions and dropping visibility to zero.

Flame enveloped the Enforcer and his motorcycle as he tried to burn his way through the thick snowstorm. For a few brief moments, he was a mobile inferno, but the snow was too thick and swirled around him too fast. He quickly had to stop or risk crashing his motorcycle at speed.

"I still think I should've blasted him," I said, glancing behind us as the snow continued forming, enveloping and blocking him from my sight. "That way we could've been sure he wouldn't chase us again."

Mel gave me a hard stare.

"Blasted him?" he asked. "With a stasis blast?"

"Yes," I said, my voice hard. "I don't think he was rushing over here to politely discuss how our surrendering to the Directorate would be the best course of action, making our lives so much better. He was going to end us. I was just being preemptive. A stasis blast would've removed him from play... hopefully permanently."

"We are *not* the Directorate," Mel said with an edge. "We are not cold-blooded, merciless murderers."

I returned his look with a hard glance of my own.

"They wouldn't hesitate to burn us to ash," I said, matching his tone. "You, of all people should know this. They blew up my home without warning. They killed Fen. They deserve no less."

"We are not them, Val," Mel repeated. "Yes, you can—and should—defend your life if it's in danger, but you've never had to *take* a life."

He became silent and looked out of his window.

After a few moments and several calming breaths, I answered him.

"How would *you* know?" I asked, gripping the wheel tight in anger. "We may share a bond, but that doesn't mean you know my entire history. It doesn't mean you know *me*."

"I know you're not a killer," he said quietly. "I would hate for you to start now."

I remained silent again and focused on the road. A swirl of emotions raged inside me. I wanted to make the Directorate pay for Fen, for destroying my home, for hating and hunting darkmages, but I knew what Fen would say: *The mission comes first. The mission always comes first.* I didn't want hate to take root, but it was becoming harder each time I faced the Directorate.

"For all they know, an ice mage just escaped apprehension," he continued. "As your Guardian, I would prefer if you allowed me to take the majority of the deadly risks—at least until your power fully manifests."

I gave him a massive dose of side-eye.

"Fen was my Guardian," I said. "He could actually...I don't mean any offense, but..."

"He could actually guard you?" Mel said, raising an eyebrow at me. "Is that what you're trying to say?"

"Well, yes, sort of," I said, glancing at him again. "You're still hurt. I mean, I get that you're my Guardian now, Fen said as much, but in your current condition, you can't do much guarding, can you? In fact, right now you're a Guardian that needs *guarding*."

"Thank you for softening the blow."

"No secrets and no smoke," I said. "We deal in honesty, right?"

"Yes," he said. "And I'm more than just your Guardian. We are bonded. You and Fen weren't."

"I don't even know what that means."

"It means that should the situation call for it, I would gladly lay my life down for you, if it meant saving yours," he said, lowering his voice. "That's what it means."

I had no doubt that Fen felt the same way, even if we weren't bonded.

"I see," I said, unsure how to react to his words. "I will try to be worthy of that kind of commitment."

He nodded.

"You will. You are."

"It doesn't mean I'm convinced about you taking all the risks, though," I said. "How about fifty-fifty?"

"Seventy-thirty," he said. "That's my only offer, which will expire once I recover, then it goes to ninety-ten."

"Ninety-ten, not one hundred?" I asked incredulously. "That's gracious of you."

"Only because one hundred percent isn't feasible without locking you in a safe house somewhere in the middle of nowhere, with round-the-clock supervision."

"No one is locking me up anywhere," I said. "Not without losing limbs and experiencing huge amounts of pain."

"Ninety-ten," he repeated. "Deal?"

"For now—yes."

"I'll take it," he said. "Where to, now? They won't give up looking for us, or rather, this vehicle."

"I know. I'm going to have to store Gladys for a bit," I said. "We are going to have to throw them off our scent for the time being, at least until things calm down a bit."

"Calm down? I don't think that's going to happen," he said. "The Directorate isn't just hunting darkmages, they're hunting anyone who is different. You just actively defied a Directorate Enforcer. We won't be able to hide for long."

"We won't need to," I said, getting off the highway. "We need a new plan to insert us into the Directorate, but first we need to go find a darkmage teacher."

"Your ice mage disguise could be a bit better," he said. "It's not very potent."

"Better?" I said. "I just stopped an Enforcer. Did you miss that part?"

"Barely," he said. "You need someone who can really help you harness your true power. As your Guardian, I can keep you safe, but I'm not a darkmage. I can't teach you what you need to learn in your stasis discipline."

"I have an address," I said. "It's the only lead I have on finding someone who can teach me."

I handed him the card Fen gave me.

"Moira Redmond?" Mel said, glancing at me. "Is this a darkmage?"

I nodded.

"I think so," I said. "Fen seemed to think she was the one who could help me when my powers started manifesting."

"We can't go downtown in this vehicle," he said, stating the obvious. "Every Enforcer in the city will be looking for it."

I swerved off the Westside Highway around 34th Street, pulling a hard right as we drove under the Jacob Javits Convention Center located on 11th Avenue.

"We're going to a convention?" he asked as I drove several levels down. He looked around, surprised, as we kept descending. "How do you even know about this place?"

"This is part of the bug-out protocol Fen created," I said. "Fen taught it to me. He made sure I knew about places like this. He had several contingency plans for emergencies. And now, you know about it too, as my Guardian."

"I'd certainly say this qualifies as an emergency," Mel said. "But I hardly think my job is to know the best places to find parking in the city."

"What exactly *is* your job?" I asked. "As you understand it, just so we're on the same page."

"My job is to keep you alive and breathing so you can grow in power until you are strong enough," he said. "I'm to help you locate the sword, the Eclipse. I'm to stand by your side, doing battle alongside you as you stand against your grandfa—Alfonse Forza, and the Directorate."

"I'm not quite there yet."

"No, you're not, but you're not alone," he said. "You have me. For now we need to hide this vehicle."

"We can hide Gladys here," I said, never taking my eyes off the ramp. "This place is perfect for that. She'll be safe."

"Where exactly is here?"

"Fen always called it the Garage," I said. "That's the only name I know for this place."

"If we leave this vehicle here, we will need another mode of transportation," he said. "I don't think it prudent to walk the streets."

"True," I said. "We would attract attention eventually."

"Do you know how to use ice magic to teleport?" he asked. "I'm just considering how we will move about. Teleportation would be ideal, but could also attract mage trackers."

"I never mastered basic ice teleportation," I said. "It's a lot more complicated than it seems."

"Understood, no teleportation," Mel said. "That limits our options somewhat."

"Okay, so teleportation is out," I said. "What do you suggest?"

"Walking, mass transit, and taxicabs," he said. "We do what we need to do to stay under the radar."

"I'm so looking forward to riding the subway," I said with thinly veiled dread. "You do know it's a breeding ground for disease and viruses, right?"

"You're a darkmage," he said as we arrived at the lowest level. "A ride in the subway isn't going to infect or kill you, I think."

"Have you ridden the subway?" I asked. "It's risking your life just getting into one of those cars. Can't we just get an Uber?"

"Of course," he said with a nod as he opened the passenger side door. With a hand, he motioned for me to exit Gladys. "Because nothing says hiding in plain sight like hiring an Uber to take us everywhere. Not like they can be tracked or anything."

"Shit," I said. "I'm just not a fan of the subway. They're moving death traps."

"We will make it work," he said. "The Directorate won't expect you to use mass transit. It gives us an advantage, even if it's a short-lived one."

"I should never have dropped my guard with Xander," I said mostly under my breath. "That was sloppy and stupid."

"Xander?"

"The Enforcer you saw who scanned me," I said. "I think that may have been him on the motorcycle."

"If it was, this has just gotten more complicated," he said. "I doubt it though."

"Why?"

"If he had scanned you and discovered you are an ice mage, or worse, a *darkmage*, you would be under arrest right now," he said. "If that was him on the motorcycle, and he had recognized you, they would have alerted several First Class Enforcers to hunt you down, snowstorm or no snowstorm."

"Because I am an ice mage?"

"Because you are an ice mage who managed to evade a direct scan," he clarified. "An ice mage who presented as normal is not by any stretch of the imagination...normal."

"I can't believe I let him scan me," I said. "He did have amazing eyes, though."

"You have feelings for this Xander?"

"Yes," I said as the rage rose in my chest. "Part of me wants to blast him to atoms, but another part of me thinks he can be saved. I don't think he's entirely evil, but he stood by and watched his brother get disintegrated. How can I forgive someone like that? Plus, he's an Enforcer. I'd like to see him and all his brothers brought to justice for what they've done to darkmages."

Mel stared at me for a few seconds.

"Tread carefully, Val, there's a fine line between love and hate."

We stepped away from the vehicle as a young man approached us and Gladys.

The young man came close to Gladys and rubbed a hand appreciatively along her hood. I could tell from his expression that he had a deep love for the car—or just cars in general.

He wore mechanic's overalls and had his long hair pulled back in a ponytail. His sharp eyes took in the both of us within moments. He gave me a short nod which I returned.

"Hello, Val," he said, looking around briefly. "Where's Fen?"

"He's not coming, Wheels," I said, the tone in my voice saying it all. "Directorate Enforcers raided the house."

"Don't count him out just yet," he said. "Fen was always tougher than he looked."

"I know."

"How can I help you?"

"We need a new ride."

"Something wrong with Gladys?" He looked at the car again. "She looks to be in great shape."

"No," I said. "We just need to disappear for a bit."

"Understood. In order to proceed, I must have the authorized passcode," he said. "Do you know it?"

I nodded.

"Fenrir, bug-out protocol 001," I said, the memory making me pause. "Succession order, Valentina 002."

"That is the correct passcode," Wheels said, serious. "I have a few options for your new ride."

"I need to blend in, but she needs to be fast, durable, and powerful."

"Got it," Wheels said, glancing at Mel. "And this is?"

"Wheels, this here is Mel, my new...my new partner," I said, motioning to Mel, standing next to me. "Mel, this is Wheels. Best driver, mechanic, and car man in the city."

Wheels tipped his head in a short nod at my words.

"A pleasure, Mel," Wheels said before turning to me. "How hot is Gladys and how long is she staying with us?"

"For the duration; right now she's too hot," I said, glancing at the automotive art that was my car. "Long stay, I'm afraid. We have some major Directorate Enforcer heat. You have a ride I can use in the short term?"

"You need to outrun Tormentors?"

I nodded.

"If it comes to that, it means I've done something wrong, but I'd like to have the power even if I don't have to use it," I answered. "What do you have for me?"

"Nothing is going to compare to Gladys," Wheels answered. "She is one of a kind, but I have a 6x6 Darkhorse built on a Bronco chassis. Just the right size for someone of your particular...personality." He gave me a once-over. "Comes fully kitted out. Not only can you outrun a Tormentor, you can run one over and come out intact on the other side with little to no damage to the Darkhorse."

"I did say I needed to disappear," I said. "A 6x6 Darkhorse sounds like the opposite of disappearing. How much speed does it have?"

"A little light on the fast department, but it is rugged, powerful, and durable."

"That sounds more like a tank," I said. "Tormentors are fast and tough. A 6x6 sounds like it's built more for durability, but not speed."

"This is faster and tougher," Wheels answered with a sly smile. "Interested?"

I crossed my arms and shook my head.

The Darkhorse sounded perfect for a head-to-head with Tormentors, but I didn't want to confront them head-on. I wanted to leave them behind, which meant I needed something durable, but fast.

"What else do you have?"

"Fen didn't want to give this to you until you were a little older," he said. "Considering the circumstances, I guess this is as good a time as any. I have a '69 Yenko Chevelle ADE."

"Is that a Chevy Chevelle?"

He nodded.

"What's the ADE stand for?"

He gave me a wicked smile.

"Anti-Directorate Edition," he answered. "Special rune-inscribed chassis, no-puncture tires made of a special polymer that simulates rubber, but has several…distinct non-rubber properties, interior and exterior runic defenses with a base in…the stasis discipline."

"A darkmage vehicle?" I asked, surprised. "How did you manage that? How was that even possible? I thought stasis was too unstable to implement defensively in a vehicle."

"So did I, until Fen convinced me otherwise," he said. "We basically made the automotive version of you."

"How?" I said, impressed. "You're not a darkmage."

"We had help. Took a long time, plenty of research and loads of secrecy," Wheels said. "Only Fen and I, and one other—whose identity I'm not allowed to divulge—know of its existence. It took me six months to design the custom matte red paint."

"Six months?"

"I dubbed it shadow paint," he said. "It was specially designed to absorb both conventional and runic tracking. If you want to disappear, this is the car to do it in."

"Has she been named?"

"Fen named her for you—Bloody Kitsune."

"The Bloody Fox?"

Wheels nodded with his smile.

"Of course blood would be involved somewhere, this is Fen," I said, shaking my head. "Why would I be surprised?"

"Want me to bring her up?"

I nodded, moved that Fen would have a vehicle created just for me.

"Please," I said. "I would like to see her."

"Up?" Mel asked, looking around "We're on the lowest level. Up from where?"

"Good eyes," Wheels said, getting behind Gladys' wheel and turning on the engine with a roar. As insanely as Fen drove her—she *was* an amazing car—I was going to miss her. "But there are always surprises in my wheelhouse. Be right back."

He stepped on the gas and drove down the length of the garage, heading straight for a wall. Mel stood transfixed, looking on at what he expected would be a totaled Gladys when Wheels drove right into the far wall.

"He's heading straight for that wall," Mel said, his voice tight with apprehension. "Unless that car is indestructible, he's going to completely destroy it, and himself, along with it."

Mel drove right though the wall, disappearing from sight.

"Everything isn't what it seems," I said.

"What the—?" he started, shocked, and looked at me. "How?"

"You can imagine my reaction the first time he did that," I said, shaking my head. "Fen chased him down and ended up bouncing off the wall...hard."

"It's a holographic wall?" Mel asked. "A runic illusion?"

"Not exactly," I said. "That wall is keyed to Gladys and his other vehicles. Wheels is a technomancer. Anything related to technology is...it's hard to explain. Tech and machines just listen to him, somehow. He can make machines respond to his will."

"He can talk to machines?" Mel asked incredulously. "Really?"

"Something like that, but deeper," I answered, still looking at the wall where Gladys vanished. "He can manipulate tech, make it do things it's not supposed to do. He's the only person Fen would trust to work on Gladys, besides Fen himself."

"So there is another level below this one?"

"There are several levels below this one," I said. "Wheels has an entire complex under the Javits. It's nearly the same size as the convention center above us, just underground."

"How did he even build something that large without getting attention?" Mel asked, surprised, as he looked around the garage. "His facility sounds enormous."

"Wheels is very connected," I said with a nod. "He knows plenty of powerful people in low places. The only vehicles he doesn't work on or provide are Directorate vehicles."

"Not a fan?"

"Directorate Enforcers killed his family in a botched op, years ago," I said, my expression grim. "He vowed never to create or work on a vehicle for the murderers of his family."

"Couldn't they just force him to?" Mel asked. "This is the Directorate we're talking about, they have massive leverage."

"Not on Wheels or his operation," I said. "Like I said, he's connected."

"Beyond connected, it seems, if he's untouchable by the Directorate."

I nodded and turned as a blood-red, angry-looking muscle car roared through the wall and headed our way. I could tell from the way Mel looked on admiringly that he approved of Kitsune.

"It suits you," Mel said, looking at the car, then glancing at me. "Both the car and the name."

Wheels rolled to a stop a few feet away and jumped out of the vehicle. True to his word, it was a beautiful, blood-red

1969 Chevy Chevelle, bristling with runic defenses. It looked mean and felt dangerous, even from a short distance.

I loved it.

SEVENTEEN

"I love it," I said, looking at Kitsune. I had shortened the name to honor Fen for the name he called me. "Are you sure we don't need something more subtle?"

"Subtle?" Wheels asked, running a hand along the side of the Kitsune. "This *is* subtle. You will blend in whether you want to or not."

He gave me a smile.

"Of course, I could always bring up the Darkhorse."

I stared at him and then smiled.

"That would be as subtle as driving around in an M1 Abrams," I said, thinking about the Darkhorse. "The Darkhorse may be a brutal work of art, but subtle, it is not."

"True. I need you to take care of her," Wheels said, pointing to Kitsune. "We only have one of these, so I took a little extra care on designing the Jankrusher array of defenses. This beauty is made to break those Janks."

"Janks?" Mel said. "What exactly are Janks?"

"It's the specific designation for the pursuit vehicles used by the Directorate—what you call the Tormentors," Wheels clarified. "They tried to merge the durability of a tank with the maneuverability of a jeep."

"Jeep-tank hybrids?" I said. "Perfect name for the defenses then, since I intend to crush every Tormentor I come across."

"Impressive," Mel said, nodding while focused on the Kitsune. "Truly a feat of engineering."

"Tormentors are nearly indestructible," Wheels continued. "Built to take massive amounts of damage and contain some of the most cutting-edge tech available, but Bloody Kitsune will keep you safe."

"Kitsune," I corrected. "Her name is Kitsune."

"And the blood in her name?"

"The Directorate will provide the blood of rage for what they did to me and my kind."

Wheels nodded silently.

"As you wish," Wheels said, tapping her hood. "I think Fen would agree. Kitsune is tough enough to deal with anything they throw at her."

"Considering what we're up against, if I can't drive it through a wall, it's too fragile," I said with a nod. "This is perfect for what I need to do in this city."

A city filled with Directorate Enforcers.

"How does it deal with energy attacks?" I asked Wheels. "Can it handle the Directorate Enforcers' flames?"

"Well, she's not indestructible," Wheels said, admiring Kitsune, "but she's damn close. If it's a rank-and-file Enforcer, it can handle the flames, even up to a First Class. You'll run into issues if it's anything higher than an Inquisitor, though."

"If we have the attention of anything higher than an Inquisitor, the last thing I'm going to be worried about is how long Kitsune is going to last," I said. "No offense."

"None taken," Wheels answered with a nod. "There are contingency plans in her in case you need to hide or escape in a hurry—active camouflage, silent running and worst-case scenario, a self-destruct array for full or partial eradication."

"I hope we never have to use that last one."

"You're a disciple of Fenrir the Feared," Wheels said, glancing at me. "A self-destruct—"

"No one calls him that anymore," I said, keeping my voice low. "It's just Fen, these days."

"I'm not just anyone," Wheels answered with a smile as he gazed on Kitsune. "I was there for most of the events that earned him that title. Anyway"—he turned to me—"if you make enemies the way he did, trust me, you're going to need the self-destruct option. It may be the only thing that saves your life."

I pulled out the card Fen gave me and showed it to him.

"Have you heard of her?" I asked, handing him the card. "I need to go see her."

Wheels read the name on the card and his expression darkened.

"Seeking her out now would be a bad idea—the worst actually," Wheels warned. "She abandoned her Catherine Lane address. The Directorate is looking for her...hard."

"Looking for her?" I asked, surprised. "Why?"

"She keeps executing their patrols," he said, handing back the card. "I would say they're eager to have a few violent words with her. I'm guessing it promises to be a short, deadly conversation."

"I can imagine," I said. "How has she managed to evade them?"

"She's a darkmage," he said as if that explained everything. "Getting in her orbit at this time would be a bad idea—lethal, even."

"Can't be helped," I said, moving the bags from Gladys to Kitsune, before jumping in behind the wheel and motioning for Mel to get in. "I need a darkmage that can handle teaching the Skills. Fen pointed me to her, so that's where I'm going."

"Shit, Val," Wheels said, glancing at me. "Have you grown tired of living? Directorate Enforcers will be all over you. This is a bad idea."

"Perfect," I said. "It'll give me a chance to test Kitsune's stealth capabilities."

"This is not a game," Wheels said. "If they ever find out" —he glanced at Mel—"you need to take this seriously. The Directorate kills darkmages on sight."

"I'll be careful," I said. "Do you know where Moira is? You said Catherine Lane is not viable."

"No, that address is a front," he said. "You know where she is... Think."

"She's a powerful darkmage," I said, connecting the dots and narrowing my eyes at him. "Is she at the Tombs?"

He gave me a tight smile.

"I cannot confirm nor deny where that insane darkmage is keeping herself these days," Wheels said, shaking his head. "Last I heard, that's where she was, though. Are you thinking of paying her a visit, seriously?"

"Yes."

"Word on the street is that the Directorate is planning a large scale offensive on the Tombs in the next few days."

"An offensive?"

"Echelon One Squads backed up with plenty of Enforcers," Wheels said. "They plan on burning down the area. If they can't infiltrate and control it, they will destroy it."

"Along with everyone inside," Mel said. "It's how they operate. No witnesses, no survivors, no mercy."

Wheels nodded.

"You won't get past the Directorate undetected," he said, shaking his head and running a hand along the top of

Kitsune. "She's stealthy, but I don't know if she's *that* stealthy."

"What do you mean?" I asked. "You said she can hide."

"Camouflage is not invisibility," Wheels explained. "it's blending in. The paint uses runic properties to bend light. Makes it hard to see her, but she isn't invisible. They will notice her if you get close enough. Now on any sort of tracking equipment, including tracker mages, she's as good as a ghost."

"So, she's invisible to tracking, but camouflaged to visual verification?"

"Yes, and they have all the entrances to the Tombs under surveillance. Not to mention that, if you do somehow miraculously manage to get past them without getting blown to bits, you'll still have to deal with the darkmages that don't appreciate uninvited guests to the Tombs. You'll have to prove yourself worthy to meet with her."

"That…I think I can do," I said, thinking about my recent stasis blast with Mel. "One more thing"—I put a hand around my ring—"I need to find a way inside the Directorate HQ. Undetected if possible."

He stared at me for a good five seconds, before shaking his head.

"I must've misheard," he said with a chuckle. "It sounded like you said you wanted to get *inside* the Directorate HQ."

"That's exactly what I said."

"If you want, I could end you right here," he said. "It would be faster and more merciful. Why would *you,* of all people, want to go *inside* the Directorate HQ? That is absolute suicide."

"They have something that belongs to me, and I want it back."

"What, your sanity?" he asked. "Tell me this is a joke. A bad joke in poor taste."

"I'm serious, Wheels, I need a way to get in and out—undetected," I said. "I know Fen was going to use you for my insertion."

"I'm going to tell you what I told him: sending you there is the same as killing you," Wheels answered. "This is certain death."

"I need you to plan my insertion into Directorate HQ," I said, my voice firm. "I'm going in, with or without your plan."

"At least you have a chance with my plan—slim, but it will be better than what you will come up with," he said. "When are you planning this kamikaze run?"

"As soon as you prepare it, we'll evaluate it and prep," I said, glancing at Mel. "Mel has been inside. He can confirm how viable it will be."

Mel nodded.

"It will be viable," Wheels said. "I know full well what the inside of the HQ looks like. I have all the points of egress and ingress, in addition to staging areas, choke points, and the like. I'm nearly done working on it."

He had just confirmed that Fen had been planning to send me in soon.

"How soon?"

"Give me two days to put the final touches on it," he said. "Come back here then—do *not* bring grief with you."

"I won't," I said. "In the meantime, I'll see if Moira wants to have a talk about darkmages."

Wheels shook his head.

"It's actually possible Fen made you crazier than he was," he said. "You turned out to be one scary woman. Fen would be proud. I know I am."

I smiled back and nodded as I extended a hand to Wheels.

"Thank you. It's not like I have much of a choice here," I

said. "For all I know, those Enforcers killed Fen. They're due what's coming to them."

"Allegedly," Wheels said. "They allegedly killed him."

"What are you talking about?" I asked in disbelief. "He was in our home when it exploded."

"Did you see a body?" Wheels asked as he gripped my hand. "Did you see him go down?"

"No, Directorate Enforcers stormed the house, followed by several explosions," I said. "I was gone before they all arrived."

"Did you see a body?" he repeated. "You didn't see them take him out?"

"No," I said. "Only the explosions from a distance."

Wheels smiled.

"I wouldn't start grieving for him just yet," he said. "That old goat is damn hard to kill."

"I'll keep that in mind. I still have to go to the Tombs," I said. "Moira might be able to help me."

"To an early and permanent retirement," he said. "How are you armed? I mean, beside your ability and"—he glanced at Mel—"is he your security?"

"Something like that," I said and showed him Stinger and the Needles. "I have these."

"Fen gave you the Needles *and* Gladys?" Wheels asked, a little surprised. "That...is a little surprising. He never let anyone hold the Needles for him...ever. Still, don't lose hope. You may have to return them to him one day."

"I hope so," I said, my voice grim. "Thank you, Wheels. Until the next."

"Until the next," Wheels answered and stepped back. "Over there"—he pointed to a section of the dash—"she's keyed to your energy signature. No one else will be able to drive her. If anyone tries, she locks down and activates the defenses."

I glanced at Mel.

"I need him to be able to drive her," I said. "How do we make that happen?"

Wheels looked at the both of us and nodded after a few seconds.

"It should be possible," he said. "You two share a bond. Through that bond, the runes on Kitsune will allow him to drive her. If that bond is ever broken though, all bets are off. She won't recognize him."

"Good to know," I said, placing my hand on the dash. Runes bloomed to life as the engine started with a throaty roar, then settled into a rumbling purr. "Anything else I need to know?"

"Plenty," he said, pointing to the large glove compartment. "It's all in the manual. Read it, learn it, memorize it. It could save your life one day."

"Will do," I said. "Thank you, again."

"Don't thank me," he said. "Just don't get dead."

I nodded as he stepped back and we roared out of the Garage.

EIGHTEEN

"The Tombs?" Mel asked. "Is that where we're going? Doesn't exactly sound like a pleasant place."

"It's not," I said. "It's rumored to be the largest concentration of darkmages in the city."

"The *largest* concentration?" Mel asked. "Why hasn't the Directorate destroyed this place yet?"

"They've tried. It's a lot easier said than done," I said. "The Tombs is a network of tunnels and spaces under the city. A literal underground city. It connects old sewer tunnels with the subway, both current and abandoned. It runs the length of the entire city. How would they go about destroying something like that?"

"The Directorate has resources, though I don't know if they have enough for an undertaking of that magnitude," Mel said. "The entire city? Something that large begs to be destroyed by them. They don't tolerate any competition well."

"Or at all," I said. "According to Wheels, it seems they plan on doing just that soon. I can't see them taking on all of the Tombs. It's just too big. It's more likely they'll hit the hub at 42nd Street."

"This seems off," Mel said, pensive. "In all my infiltration missions for the Directorate, I was never sent into these Tombs. Why not? I would be the perfect candidate to infiltrate this place."

"Hmm," I said. "Either the Directorate didn't fully trust you, or feared they would lose you to the darkmages."

"Or both," Mel said. "Do you know anything about this Moira?"

"Only that according to Fen, once my abilities started manifesting, I needed to see her," I said. "Other than that, I don't know much else."

"This is dangerous," Mel said. "We're heading into potentially dangerous—"

"Not potentially," I said. "These darkmages don't know who I am, and I don't plan on revealing myself to anyone besides Moira down there."

"They will see you as a hostile."

"What do you think they will view you as?" I asked. "Nice, warm and friendly?"

"I am neither warm nor friendly, and I don't do nice," he said. "I think this is a bad idea. Do you even know what this Moira looks like?"

"No."

"So what's the plan?" Mel asked. "You run the Directorate gauntlet, hope to survive that ordeal only to confront a group of hostile darkmages and do what? Ask around for Moira to see if she is available to see some rogue ice mage?"

"I'm open to suggestions," I said. "Do you have the address of any darkmage instructors taking students?"

"Of course not," he snapped. "Advertising something like that would be an instant death sentence."

"Then this is the best option I have," I said. "We go to the Tombs and hopefully this Moira will see me."

"And if she doesn't?"

"It's no coincidence that this place was named the Tombs," I said. "If she won't see me the easy way, we'll have to do it the hard way."

We sped out of the Javits Convention Center.

I headed straight on 36th Street, and turned left onto 8th Avenue, and headed uptown.

"Where exactly is the entrance to these Tombs located?" Mel asked, looking around to see if there were any Tormentors around us. "It seems we've lost the Directorate for now."

"Port Authority Bus Terminal building, or rather *under* it," I said. "That is the main entrance, but I hear there are hundreds, if not thousands of entrances, scattered throughout the city."

"The Port Authority Bus Terminal, on 42nd Street?" Mel asked incredulously. "The one located on one of the busiest intersections of the city? That Port Authority?"

"625 8th Avenue," I said, keeping one eye on the traffic behind us. Wheels may be proud of Kitsune's stealth capabilities, but to me, they were still unproven tech. "As far as I know, there's only one located in the city, like I said. It's not in that building but—"

"Under it," Mel finished. "And this is common knowledge?"

"Yes," I said, avoiding traffic. "Why does that surprise you?"

"I find it staggering that such a threat could exist in plain sight and no action has been taken by their enemy."

"A threat?" I asked, my words decidedly chilly. "Are you referring to darkmages as the threat in this case?"

"According to the Directorate, they perceive them as

threat," he said, measuring his words. "I meant no offense to you personally."

"Some taken."

"My apologies," he said with a short nod. "I just don't understand it."

"It's not hard to understand," I said. "What do darkmages do?"

"Darkmages die," he said. "Everyone knows that."

"That's just it," I said, slowing our approach to 42nd Street as I noticed the increase of stationary Tormentors on either side of 8th Avenue. They really were gearing up for an assault. "How long do you think it took the Directorate to make that the accepted position against darkmages? Even *you* just called us a threat."

"Not deliberately."

"That's the point," I said. "If the Directorate can make that the accepted truth, they can eliminate us at their leisure. Who's going to complain?"

"No one," he said after a pause. "There will be no darkmage uprising, because even the darkmages are splintered. They distrust even each other."

"Exactly. There's no rush to wipe us out because they have everyone convinced that darkmages die. What other options do we have? Everyone views us as a threat, a danger to society, worthy of death. All darkmages do is corrupt and destroy. They're doing us a favor by killing us."

"It's an insidious and deeply rooted belief system they have created," Mel said, shaking his head. "Fomenting this thought process must have taken a concerted effort over decades."

"Longer, I think," I said. "And it works. People fear what they don't understand, and it's a small step from fear to hate. The Directorate did their job well."

"The real question is why?" Mel asked. "Why this

campaign against the darkmages? To my knowledge, outside of your grandfather, who actively stood against and fought the Directorate, darkmages posed no overt threat to the Directorate or society at large. Why target them for eradication?"

"It's in the potential," I said, thinking back to my conversation with Fen. "Darkmages pose a threat—that much is true. If we ever managed to unite, we could topple the Directorate."

"I'm certain that possibility gives the Pentarch sleepless nights."

"I sure hope so," I said, slowing even further as more Directorate forces were gathering around the entrance to the Tombs. "Wheels underreported what was happening here. This is a major assault."

"They certainly look determined," Mel said, looking out of his window. "I still can't believe the entrance to the Tombs is common knowledge."

"Most of the magic authorities in the city know where the entrance to the Tombs is located. Getting in is not the issue."

"Then what is?"

"Entering the Tombs is almost encouraged," I said. "Getting in is easy; getting out alive, that's an entirely different matter. Although after our little drive this morning, getting in may be harder than usual."

"We're in for a world of pain, aren't we?"

"Pain lets you know you're alive.

I turned on 42nd Street and saw the ramp that led to the lower levels of the Port Authority. Stationed just in front of the ramp were several Tormentors creating an unofficial checkpoint.

Any vehicle going into the building was being stopped.

I paused for about a minute, creating a lag in the line entering the building. When we had enough room ahead, I floored the accelerator and prayed Wheels wasn't exaggerating about Kitsune's defenses as we sped forward.

Gunfire erupted behind us almost immediately.

A pair of Tormentors, parked nose to nose in a staggered formation blocked our path to the ramp and the lower levels of the Tombs.

I flipped a large red switch labeled JKD on the dash and hoped the initials meant Jankrusher Defenses.

Runes inside the Kitsune flared to life, bathing the interior in a deep blue fluorescent glow. I felt the entire vehicle lower itself closer to the ground, as if it were hunkering down. There were several other sounds I couldn't identify, but was certain had some part in our surviving the next few seconds.

We collided with the first Tormentor.

Kitsune impacted the side of the Tormentor and shunted it to one side effortlessly. What I was witnessing shouldn't have been possible. The Tormentor easily outweighed Kitsune, which had shoved the much larger vehicle to one side as if it had been made of thin aluminum and not steel.

Several Directorate mages unleashed orbs of destruction at us. Thankfully none of them were Inquisitors so their orbs bounced off Kitsune harmlessly.

Mel looked on in wonder as the orbs impacted and did no damage. I was impressed, but had no time to enjoy the spectacle as a waiting Tormentor rammed us from behind and shoved us.

Apparently, the defenses could be overwhelmed momentarily. Granted, that hit should have totaled Kitsune, which it didn't, but the force of the blow slammed us against the wall of the ramp. The runes on Kitsune acted as a force dampener, distributing the energy over the larger surface of the car.

I corrected our trajectory and continued down the ramp while accelerating. I was definitely going too fast.

The Tormentor closed again, trying for another ramming run.

"Watch out!" Mel yelled. "He's going to try and hit us again!"

I let him get close and at the last possible second, said a silent prayer to Wheels, hoping he really added extra defenses to Kitsune as the Tormentor rammed us again, launching us across the ramp, making us briefly airborne.

I looked ahead as the bottommost level of the ramp rushed up at us. Fortunately, we were falling flat, which, if I had to pick the lesser of evils, falling flat was better than falling nose first, or on our back.

It was still falling several levels down into the Tombs.

"This can't be good," Mel said, looking out of his window as the lower ramp level far below us grew closer. If Wheels' defenses were subpar, we were going to be buried in what remained of Kitsune after we landed. "Isn't there some switch for situations like this?"

I stared at him and almost laughed.

"I don't think Wheels put in an aerial landing switch," I said. "Hold on!"

We landed hard and bounced once before coming to a stop near the far wall at the end of the ramp. A group of figures immediately surrounded Kitsune, encouraging me to keep the doors locked and remain inside the vehicle.

Somehow the landing wasn't as jarring as I'd expected. I'd actually expected Kitsune to end up scattered as debris, along with our broken bodies.

"They were waiting for us," Mel said. "And they don't look happy."

"I can't believe Kitsune survived that drop," I said, keeping my voice low. An array of runes raced along the interior, giving me the feeling of being inside a strobe light. After a few seconds, it calmed down to a slow pulse and a few moments after, even that died down. "I don't know how Wheels did it, but I'm glad he did."

"I second that," Mel said with a slight groan. "Do we want to greet our hosts?"

He pointed outside to the group of people assembled outside of Kitsune. Most of them were dressed simply—plain clothing without any distinctive features. Some of them tentatively touched Kitsune and pulled their hands back as if burned.

Three of them wore black cloaks over combat armor and approached the driver's side. One of the black-cloaked, a woman, stepped close to Kitsune and lightly tapped the driver's side window.

"I think they want us to come outside," I said, nodding at the woman. "Well, it's not like we can stay in here indefinitely."

"Actually, we probably can," Mel said, before I shot him a look. "But it may be better if we go outside and find out what they want."

"Good idea," I said, opening my door. "Let's go."

NINETEEN

I stepped outside and the woman who stood in front of my door stepped back a few paces. The two men beside her formed orbs of black energy.

They were darkmages.

Despite his reluctance at leaving the car, Mel appeared at my side a few moments later, showing no signs of fear.

"My name is Cleve," she said. "State your purpose for entering the Tombs unbidden."

There was no point in lying. We were surrounded by darkmages. If there was one thing they would be able to do, it was see through a lie. I opted for honesty.

"I'm here to see Moira," I said, facing Cleve. "Can you take us to her?"

Some of the darkmages gathered around us shook their heads. Others laughed. Cleve and her guards only hardened their expressions.

"Moira doesn't see guests," Cleve said. "Why should she see you?"

I could go with my ice mage disguise plan, but somehow, I knew it wouldn't work. They would turn me down and eject me from the Tombs with extreme prejudice—right into the arms of the waiting Directorate outside.

"I need a darkmage to teach me the Skills," I said, sounding more confident than I felt. "I was told to seek her out, that she could show me what I needed to know."

Now all except Cleve and her guards laughed at me.

"Not exactly the reaction I was expecting," Mel said under his breath. "Nonetheless, it's better than drawn weapons and overt attacks."

Even Cleve gave me a tight smile as she shook her head.

"You're either brave or suicidal," Cleve said, her expression skeptical with a hint of admiration. "You're a darkmage?"

"Yes."

"What House?" Cleve asked, serious. "What House do you belong to?"

Fen had taught me that long ago darkmages, before being persecuted for merely existing, had been organized into Houses—families who wielded power and influence.

Though it wasn't as organized now, every darkmage theoretically could trace their lineage back to one of the twelve Houses. My grandfather was the head of ours, House Forza, the smallest and yet most powerful of the Houses.

Once I shared this, I had a feeling things would go sideways.

"House Forza," I said without raising my voice. "I belong to House Forza."

"Liar," I heard from several of the people around us. "She's a spy. Kill her."

Cleve's expression darkened as she glanced around.

"We do not commit unprovoked murder," she said. "That would make us no better than the dogs at our door. Is that who we are?"

The crowd murmured a few no's and shot me some dirty

looks. Most of them appeared to be properly chastised, but none of them left. I had become a novelty.

Cleve turned to me.

"You claim to be a darkmage," she said, giving me a hard stare, "but you barely read as a mage. Why shouldn't I have my men just release you to the Directorate and keep your vehicle?"

"You could," I said, returning her stare. "It would be a mistake and I would hate to break your men."

Both men glared at me.

It was easy to underestimate me. I wasn't very tall or muscular. Currently, my energy signature wasn't broadcasting any significant amount of power. As far as they knew, I was some low-level mage with a death wish.

"Can you prove your claim?" Cleve asked, still staring at me. "Alfonse Forza, along with most of his House, has all but vanished from existence. It's a convenient choice, but I'm going to need more than your word. Can you prove your House?"

"To Moira, yes," I said. "And *only* to her."

"This could be a ploy," the guard on her left said. "She could be a Directorate assassin sent here to remove Moira."

"Unlikely," Cleve said without taking her eyes off me. "Directorate assassins are far more subtle"—she glanced at Mel—"like that changeling, there. Though, he's bonded to her. No, they're not assassins. What they are, however, is a mystery."

Mel's eyes widened in surprise, but he remained silent.

Cleve narrowed her eyes at me and leaned in. The two guards next to her were tense and looked ready to blast me back up the ramp to the Directorate.

"You have no idea what you're asking," Cleve said. "Moira leads a large faction of us in the Tombs."

"Does she lead a House?"

"No, but she holds the same level of authority," Cleve said. "You don't just show up and demand to see her. I don't care who you claim to be, it's not done."

"I'm not leaving here without seeing her," I said. "You have no idea what I went through to get here."

"Nor do I care," Cleve said and looked to her left and right. "Escort them to the Directorate upstairs, and leave my new car in the garage."

She turned to leave.

"You're making a mistake."

She stopped and turned to face me.

"No, you made a mistake when you decided to come down that ramp," Cleve said, pointing at my chest. "No darkmage would attempt to see Moira without a formal introduction. That tells me a few things about you. You're not from a formal House, more likely a rogue from some unknown splinter."

"You're wrong," I said, keeping my anger in check. "My claim is true."

"Sure it is," Cleve said, dismissing my words. "A *real* member of House Forza would read as a darkmage, a powerful darkmage, not whatever you are. Like I said, convenient choice—it's nearly impossible to corroborate—but also a stupid one. House Forza possessed some of the most powerful darkmages of all of the Houses. You are *not* a Forza darkmage."

"I am—"

"Save it," Cleve said, raising a hand. "It's a good story, but it is full of holes. Holes big enough to drive a Tormentor through. But thanks for the car." She looked at her guards again. "Get them out of my sight. We have enough to worry about with the Directorate Hounds upstairs. I don't have time for pretend mages chasing delusions of grandeur."

She started walking away and I felt Mel begin to transform. His hands grew and his fingernails elongated into sharp claws.

So much for my question about his weapons.

He is a weapon.

I placed a hand on his shoulder and shook my head.

"Let me deal with this," I said. "These are my people. It shouldn't be an issue if I unleash my power in here. After all, almost everyone in the Tombs is a darkmage."

He nodded and stepped back as I saw his hands revert back to normal. I removed the ring from the chain around my neck and placed it on my finger. Raw power flowed through my body as the ring tightened around my finger. The runes on the chain blazed with orange light before growing dim.

I placed the chain in a pocket and faced the guards as Mel stepped close to my side.

"Those were obfuscation runes," Mel said. "Every Directorate Mage above us is going to sense that energy spike."

"Yes, apparently my word wasn't proof enough," I said. "So we're going to try a different method."

Cleve stopped in her tracks and turned to face me.

"If they were thinking of an assault before, you've practically guaranteed it now," Mel said. "They will recognize that energy signature."

"I tried to do this the easy way," I said, never taking my eyes off Cleve. "She wanted hard, now we do it hard."

"Who are you?" Cleve asked as she formed a deep blue orb of power. "That power you're wielding, it's not yours. I will ask one more time. Who are you?"

"I am Valentina Forza," I said, drawing the Needles. "This power is my birthright. I am the granddaughter of Alfonse Forza, the bane of the Directorate, and one of the most powerful darkmages to walk this earth."

I let the power flow through me and could feel my hair turning white as black energy formed around my body.

That's when all hell broke loose.

TWENTY

Squadrons of Enforcers raced down the ramp, and with them, blasts of living flame.

"They're only darkmages. Kill them all, but leave the white-haired one to me," a voice said over the chaos. "I want her alive. I will make you wish you had died several times if she's killed before I interview her."

I recognized the voice.

Enforcer Holland.

Which meant that Ashford couldn't be too far away. Those two always patrolled together. It would make sense for Ashford to be close, maybe even on this floor.

Interview—I knew the kinds of interviews Holland conducted. If I let it get that far, my chance of survival dropped to zero. From the shadows, dozens of darkmages emerged, firing orbs of power back at the Enforcers.

The darkmages were outnumbered for now, but we were in the Tombs. The numbers advantage would turn soon. The ring pulsed on my hand with darkmage energy as Cleve drew close, staring at my hand.

"You crazy bitch," Cleve said as she drew close with a

wicked grin. "You could have just showed me the ring. I could have verified who you were with a scan."

"Oh," I said. "I didn't think—"

"Damn straight you didn't think," Cleve said, forming a shield and deflecting several orbs. "Now you've started a war the Directorate won't walk away from—not until they take you into custody, or make you a corpse."

"What are you talking about?"

"Not here, and not now," Cleve said, ducking under an orb and firing several of her own. "You need to go down." She whistled a high-pitched tone. "They'll take you down to see her."

"Who?" I asked, confused, since I didn't see anyone. "Take me down to see who?"

"Are you always this dense?" Cleve snapped. "You wanted to see Moira. They will take you to her. Go now! The Dark Aegis will take you to her."

Five guards materialized around me and Mel.

They all wore the same combat armor as Cleve, without the cloaks. On each of their right shoulders, I saw the emblem of a rearing blue lion, with flames all around its body.

Their faces were hidden by masks, and in each of their hands they held a short sword that gave off a distinct blue glow. The lead guard of the five stepped forward and placed a hand across his chest.

"Please, come with us," he said. "My name is Byron Redmond. I will take you to see Moira."

"Redmond?" I asked. "Are you related—?"

"She's my aunt," he said with a quick nod, before looking behind us. "Cleve, the defenses are collapsing. Can you shore them up while I escort Ms. Forza to the lower levels?"

"Get her out of here," Cleve said. "I'll hold the Directorate for as long as it takes, before I give the fade out signal."

"I'm counting on you," Byron said.

"What else is new?" Cleve shot back with grin. "Get her off this level."

He motioned with a nod and the other four fanned out around us. He pointed forward, deeper into the Tombs. Behind us, the sounds of battle were raging. I glanced back and saw Michael battling several darkmages at once.

They were no match for him.

They were holding their own, but he would soon overpower them. Behind him, I saw more squads of Enforcers rushing in to reinforce their ranks.

The darkmages couldn't hold this position for much longer.

"Miss," Byron said, placing a hand on my arm and snapping me out of my thoughts, "we must leave now."

I nodded and made sure Mel was close. Not that I needed to. He was standing close to my side.

"This took a turn for the violent in a hurry," Mel said. "I've never seen the Directorate this feral before. I can't explain it."

"No need," Byron said. "We can discuss this later." He turned to Cleve. "I need ten seconds, can you manage it?"

"Why are you still here talking?" Cleve barked at him. "Get off my level!"

"Hurry," Byron said and took off at a run deeper into the Tombs, with Mel and me following him. His other guards were immediately behind us. I couldn't see or hear them, but I could sense them nearby. "This way."

Byron turned into one of the many dark tunnels that branched off the main area. We had to enter the tunnel single-file, with Byron in the lead. Mel and I were right behind him, and the rest of the guards brought up the rear.

We ran for what seemed like miles.

The sounds of battle diminished behind us until all I

heard was our breathing as we kept moving. Eventually, everything was quiet, but we weren't alone.

All around us, I could sense mages.

Darkmages.

We were in a dimly lit atrium with balconies along each of the walls. In the center, I saw three large chairs. Two of the chairs were unoccupied, but a woman sat in the center chair.

I couldn't make out her features clearly, but I could sense the weight of power from her energy signature. She was a darkmage, one who commanded vast amounts of power.

Byron stepped forward and placed a hand across his chest.

"As instructed," he said and motioned to me with an arm. "The catalyst."

"The what?" I said, confused. "What did you call me?"

"You are the reason for the uproar above?" the woman said and gazed at me, her eyes flashing violet. She shook her head and smiled at me. It was a sad smile. "Of course you are." She motioned me to her with a hand. "Come closer, child. I would look upon Alfonse's legacy."

I stepped closer, expecting Byron and Mel to stay by my side, but they left me alone to approach the woman.

Her long, gray hair was pulled back into a loose ponytail. Her eyes flashed violet every few seconds as subtle waves of power came off of her. She wore black combat armor identical to Byron's, except her right shoulder held a golden lion.

"Moira?" I asked. "Are you Moira?"

"Yes," she said, her strong, melodious voice filling the atrium. "I hear you wanted to see me?"

"I did, I mean I do," I answered. "Fen said I needed to see you."

"Did he now?" she said, raising an eyebrow. "Did he tell you to start a major conflict between the Directorate and my people in the process?"

"Well, no," I said, evading her gaze. "That was...I mean, I didn't know. I'm sorry, I didn't mean to start that conflict."

"How is Fenrir?" she asked, her voice a little softer. "Is he still incorrigible?"

"He, well, Enforcers attacked the house," I explained. "There were explosions and—"

"I understand," Moira said. "You wouldn't be here otherwise. I sense your heart is heavy at this loss. Don't grieve him just yet. Fenrir has proven incredibly difficult to eliminate in the past. I don't think rank and file Enforcers will dispatch him so easily. Now, child, why did you want to see me?"

"Fen said I needed to see you when my powers began to manifest," I explained. "My powers blasted Mel and—"

"Mel?" Moira asked. "Who is Mel?"

I glanced over at Mel.

"Ah, I see, the changeling," Moira said. "Please come forward, Mel."

Mel stepped forward and stood next to me.

"It has been some time since I have spoken to one of your kind," Moira said, as her eyes flashed violet again. "You are bonded to her. To what purpose?"

"I am her Guardian," Mel said, looking Moira in the eyes. "To the last breath if need be."

"Hers or yours?"

"Mine," he answered. "My purpose is to ensure she becomes strong enough to wield the Eclipse and stop Alfonse Forza."

"No small task," Moria said. "Why are you here? I do not possess the Eclipse."

"But you possess knowledge," I said. "If I may be so bold, would you teach me the Skills?"

Moira smiled before shaking her head slowly.

"No, I'm afraid not," Moira said and my heart sank. "You need an actual darkmage instructor."

"I don't understand. Why would Fen send me to see you?"

"He didn't," Moira said. "Fen only passed on the message. The one who sent you to see me has a deeper, more complex scheme in motion."

"I don't understand."

"And you won't for some time," Moira said. "But there was a purpose in sending you to me. I may not be able to teach you, but I know who can."

"You do?"

"Yes, but before I give you her name, you must be certain you want to walk this path," Moira said. "Once you set upon it, there is no turning back. You must give yourself completely to your purpose. Can you do that?"

"I can."

"I sense a conflict in your heart, young Forza," Moira said. "You must be single-minded of purpose. There will be no room for doubt in this. Do you understand?"

"I do. I need to find the Eclipse and I need to stop the Directorate."

"You may also need to stand against your grandfather one day," Moira warned. "Do you think you are capable?"

"I will do what I have to do to keep darkmages safe," I said. "If that means standing against Alfonse Forza, then I will."

"Very well," Moira said. "Your words are your bond and have been witnessed by myself and those around you. May you have the strength to fulfill them."

"Who must I see?"

"In the far reaches of the Tombs lies a teacher of the Skills," Moira said. "She is revered and feared. No one dares to enter her domain for fear of her reprisals. Her name is Alala the Piercing. She can teach you the Skills, if she doesn't kill you first. It has been a long time since she had a disciple."

"Don't all darkmages learn the Skills?"

"No, child," Moira said with a smile. "To request the Skills is to undergo the most rigorous and deadly of darkmage teachings. Only those born in direct lineage to one of the twelve Houses can even make the request. You have been set on a path of pain and destruction."

"That sounds like my life so far."

She looked up and away for a few seconds before returning her gaze to me.

"You must leave now, but I will not send you away unarmed," Moira said. "By placing that ring on your hand, you have uncovered your energy signature."

"I still have the chain," I said. "I can just"—I reached into my pocket and pulled out the chain. It turned black and crumbled to dust as I held it up to show her—"Nevermind. I thought I had obfuscation runes so I could hide."

"You do," she said, standing. "Extend your hand."

I held out my hand.

She closed her eyes for a second as her hand glowed a deep blue. The next moment, she traced a symbol in my hand. The blue energy enveloped me and expanded to cover Mel too.

"What is that?"

"A particular obfuscation rune," she said. "Learn the symbol, it will serve you well in the future. Especially when you retrieve your birthright."

"My birthright?"

"You'll understand soon," she said. "For now, you must go. The Enforcers are coming and bring death in their wake. This attack on the Tombs will result in casualties for both sides. They will leave here defeated, but not deterred. They will hunt you now. You must get stronger, *Shiroi Kitsune*—White Fox."

"I will," I said. "Thank you, Moira."

"You are most welcome," she said. "Perhaps, one day, we

will sit and enjoy a time free from persecution. Until that time, you must become the blade to stand against those who would kill darkmages."

Moira gave Byron a look.

He nodded in return and turned to me.

"This way," he said as the four other guards around him snapped to attention. "I will take you to your car and the nearest exit from the Tombs."

"Is it safe?"

"Today, no place is safe in the Tombs," he said. "But, it's safer than this place will be in a few minutes. Let's go."

He bowed to Moira.

I did the same and noticed that Mel had followed Byron's example. Moira bowed back to us and then nodded. Byron glanced at his guards who formed up behind us. He took off at a run and we left the atrium.

TWENTY ONE

We wound our way through tunnels and passageways until I was hopelessly lost. We continued, following Byron until he led us to an underground chamber with an exit large enough to fit a bus.

Sitting alongside the far wall, I saw Kitsune.

"You can't stay here long," Byron said, glancing over his shoulder. "Enforcers are everywhere. I had to take a complicated route just to buy us the few minutes you now have—don't squander them."

"We won't," I said. "Thank you."

"None needed," Byron said. "We are darkmages. We are one."

With a gesture, he and his four guards disappeared.

"An impressive exit," Mel said, sniffing the air as we headed toward Kitsune. "The sooner we are out of these Tombs, the better."

"Agreed," I said. "We need to get back to—"

The energy signature filled the room, and I stopped walking... turning slowly to face the Enforcer that I knew was behind us.

"Stop where you are," he said, forming an orb of flame. "I don't want to use force, but I will if you don't comply."

I turned and stared into Xander Ashford's eyes.

"Comply," I said. "You mean surrender."

He stared at me and I shook my head, letting my bright white hair partially block my face.

"Do I know you?" he asked. "You look famil—"

"All darkmages look alike," I said, cutting him off. "We only exist to be exterminated, right?"

"I didn't say—"

"You didn't have to," I said. "Darkmages die. Isn't that what you Enforcers say? My kind are worthless to you. A blight on society, worthy only of extermination."

"Where did you hear those words?" he asked, pointing at me. "I never said those words."

"You want me to comply so your other Enforcer friends can get here, and then what? I'm executed?"

"We're not monsters," he said. "We don't—"

"Liar," I said. "How many did you kill getting here?"

"None," he said defiantly. "I was tracking a particular energy signature. A normal that shouldn't have been down here, but that's clearly not you. I got turned around in these tunnels. I haven't run into anyone—until you."

Tracking a normal energy signature. He was tracking me.

"Your Enforcer brothers aren't showing mercy upstairs," I said as I started taking slow steps back toward Kitsune. "Many darkmages will die today."

His expression hardened.

"So will Enforcers," he said. "Are their lives less valuable?"

"Are you trying to justify darkmage deaths?" I asked. "Are darkmages hunting *you* down?"

"No," he said. "That could never happen."

"Are we eliminating you just for existing?" I asked. "The

way the Directorate has issued a death sentence for all of my kind?"

"No," he said. "Stop moving. I wish it wasn't this way, but this is how it is, how it's always been. Stand still or I will be forced to unleash this orb. You will not survive a direct hit."

"Empty words," I scoffed as the rage rose in my chest. "It's easy to wish things were different when you're the one with the power. All of you Enforcers are alike."

"No, we aren't," he said. "Not all of us."

"From where I'm standing, Mr. 'Comply or I'll be forced to barbecue you', you're certainly acting like every other Enforcer."

I glanced at Mel who was now closer to Kitsune than I was and gave him a subtle nod and glanced at the driver's side. I hoped he understood that I wanted him to get to Kitsune and get her ready to beat a hasty retreat.

There was no way we could stand against the several squads of Enforcers headed our way. Especially not with Holland leading them. Mel nodded back and I really hoped he got my message.

With a quick shift of my weight, I drew Stinger from its holster and aimed it at Xander's head. I had trained for countless hours to gain the speed I had. In half a second, I had him in my sights.

"Absorb your orb," I said. "Or this becomes the last conversation you have…ever."

"You're fast," he said admiringly. "I didn't expect that."

"I'm sure there's plenty you don't expect from darkmages."

The orb he held in his hand disappeared a second later, much to my surprise.

"Now what?" he asked. "You were right. My Enforcer brothers are coming. They'll be here any minute. When they get here, you plan on shooting all of us? It's just you two against hundreds of Enforcers."

"I don't need to shoot all of you—just you."

"Proving what the Directorate says about darkmages," he said. "You're all just cold-blooded killers deserving of death. Is that what you are?"

"If that was who I was, I'd be looking at a corpse," I said as I felt another energy spike. We were out of time. "I'd really like to continue this conversation, but it's time for me to go —Xander."

"What?" he said, shocked. "How do you know—?"

I took advantage of his momentary shock to turn and dash toward Kitsune, as Mel turned the engine on with a roar and shoved open the passenger side door with a kick. Behind Xander, Holland and a squad of Enforcers jumped into the room from a side tunnel, unleashing flame orbs in our direction.

I dove into Kitsune, narrowly avoiding being flambéed as I slammed the door closed behind me.

"Go!" I yelled. "Now!"

Mel floored the accelerator as the flame orbs harmlessly bounced off Kitsune. We raced down the tunnel, leaving the Enforcers behind. I looked in the rear-view mirror to see Holland screaming at Xander.

That wasn't going to end well.

I leaned my head back against the seat and closed my eyes.

"Where to?" Mel asked as we surfaced on 10th Avenue and 49th Street. "I strongly suggest we avoid midtown for the duration of the evening."

"Good idea," I said, thinking. We had some time before Wheels would have our infiltration plan ready. By now, the Directorate would have abandoned my home, leaving it a charred husk. There's no way they would've discovered Fen's library. "Let's go home, there are some books I need."

"Are you sure that's prudent?" Mel asked. "There may still be a Directorate presence on the property."

"We'll do a recon drive-by to make sure the place is clear," I said, looking out of the window. "I have a feeling with all this activity at the Tombs, they'll be too busy to pay attention to an insignificant home in the Village."

"You may be right," Mel said. "But just to be on the safe side, I'll change into another form and scout the property first, *before* you go in. Deal?"

"Deal," I said with a tired nod. "Let's go see what the Directorate left of my past."

We drove off into the night and headed home.

END of BOOK ONE

AUTHOR NOTES

Thank you for reading this story and jumping into the world of Darkmages with me.

Disclaimer:

The Author Notes are written at the very end of the writing process.

This section is not seen by the ART or my amazing Jeditor.

Any typos or errors following this disclaimer are mine and mine alone.

I was never going to attempt writing anything with romance.

I call those—famous last words.

I have learned in most of my writing to never say never. It took a while with an attempt at romance, but it happened, eventually. Even with this story, I'm leaning heavier on the urban fantasy side, but there aspects of romance that I would hesitate to put in my other stories.

I ask that you be patient with me, as I write this series, I'm learning what makes this hybrid genre tick. There will certainly be growing pains as I dive into this world. With that said, I know my readers will not be shy about informing me if something works or not. I'm counting on you as readers to help me make these stories excellent.

Regarding the story, there is much character development to come.

Val has to grow into her power and even though they share a bond, Val and Mel still have to grow in their respective roles. I know I didn't go in-depth into what a changeling is or how they, well, change. I promise to explore it further in the next book.

I also have to enhance the interaction between Val and Xander and somehow get them to really dislike each other before any spark of attraction can blossom between them. Love and hate are two sides of the same coin in these stories. Having characters travel the spectrum from one to the other successfully is what makes a story worth reading.

The antagonist and villain are certainly in place. They are not the same person and there is also the entity of the Directorate and Pentarch. All those promise to be fun to explore and develop. There is still much for me to learn, even there, these villains will be complicated with agendas and machinations that will impact the relationships Val has.

Speaking of relationships, let's discuss Fen.

As Wheels and Moira said, Fen is a hard target, and killing him is no easy feat. Is he dead? We'll find out. I don't want to spoil anything and his absence right now, gives Val room to grow. I have a feeling he may pay her a visit later on as he watches her from the shadows.

Which leads to the character that we all know is inevitable—Alfonse Forza.

Eventually, Val will have to confront her grandfather and her family. This conflict is one of the driving forces of the series. Val will have to grow in strength and wisdom to face off against one of the most powerful darkmages to roam the Earth.

She will have help, she will increase in her power, she will make mistakes, and she will transform. I hope you join me in this new adventure as we watch her face-off against those will try to subvert her power for their own hidden agendas and those who would destroy her for being a darkmage.

Thank you so much for reading this story and making the space for me to explore a new world with new characters. I look forward for walking this path alongside you.

Thank you again for jumping into this story with me!

SUPPORT US

Patreon
The Magick Squad

Website/Newsletter
www.orlandoasanchez.com

JOIN US

Facebook
Montague & Strong Case Files

Youtube
Bitten Peaches Publishing Storyteller

Instagram
bittenpeaches

Email
orlando@orlandoasanchez.com

M&S World Store
Emandes

BITTEN PEACHES PUBLISHING

Thanks for Reading!
If you enjoyed this book, would you please **leave a review** at the site you purchased it from? It doesn't have to be long… just a line or two would be fantastic and it would really help me out.

Bitten Peaches Publishing offers more books and audiobooks
across various genres including: urban fantasy, science fiction, adventure, & mystery!

www.BittenPeachesPublishing.com

More books by Orlando A. Sanchez

Montague & Strong Detective Agency Novels
Tombyards & Butterflies•Full Moon Howl•Blood is Thicker•Silver Clouds Dirty Sky•Homecoming•Dragons & Demigods•Bullets & Blades•Hell Hath No Fury•Reaping Wind•The Golem•Dark Glass•Walking the

Razor•Requiem•Divine Intervention•Storm Blood•Revenant•Blood Lessons•Broken Magic•Lost Runes•Archmage•Entropy•Corpse Road•Immortal

Montague & Strong Detective Agency Stories
No God is Safe•The Date•The War Mage•A Proper Hellhound•The Perfect Cup•Saving Mr. K

Night Warden Novels
Wander•ShadowStrut•Nocturne Melody

Rule of the Council
Blood Ascension•Blood Betrayal•Blood Rule

The Warriors of the Way
The Karashihan•The Spiritual Warriors•The Ascendants•The Fallen Warrior•The Warrior Ascendant•The Master Warrior

John Kane
The Deepest Cut•Blur

Sepia Blue
The Last Dance•Rise of the Night•Sisters•Nightmare•Nameless•Demon

Chronicles of the Modern Mystics
The Dark Flame•A Dream of Ashes

The Treadwell Supernatural Directive
The Stray Dogs•Shadow Queen•Endgame Tango

Brew & Chew Adventures
Hellhound Blues

Bangers & Mash
Bangers & Mash

Tales of the Gatekeepers
Bullet Ballet•The Way of Bug•Blood Bond

Division 13
The Operative•The Magekiller

Blackjack Chronicles
The Dread Warlock

The Assassin's Apprentice
The Birth of Death

Gideon Shepherd Thrillers
Sheepdog

DAMNED
Aftermath

Nyxia White
They Bite•They Rend•They Kill

Iker the Cleaner
Iker the Unseen•Daystrider•Nightwalker

Fate of the Darkmages
Fated Fury

Stay up to date with new releases!
Shop www.orlandoasanchez.com for more books and audiobooks!

ART SHREDDERS

I want to take a moment to extend a special thanks to the ART SHREDDERS.

No book is the work of one person. I am fortunate enough to have an amazing team of advance readers and shredders.

Thank you for giving of your time and keen eyes to provide notes, insights, answers to the questions, and corrections (dealing wonderfully with my extreme dreaded comma allergy). You help make every book and story go from good to great. Each and every one of you helped make this book fantastic, and I couldn't do this without each of you.

THANK YOU

ART SHREDDERS

Amber, Anne Morando, Audrey Cienki
Bethany Showell, Beverly Collie
Carrie Anne O'Leary, Chris Christman II
Denise King, Diane Craig, Donna Young Hatridge

Hal Bass

Jasmine Breeden, Jeanette Auer, Jen Cooper, Joy Kiili, Julie Peckett

Karen Hollyhead

Larry Diaz Tushman, Laura Tallman I

Malcolm Robertson, Marcia Campbell, Maryelaine Eckerle-Foster, Melissa Miller

Paige Guido, Penny Campbell-Myhill

RC Battels, Rob Farnham

Stacey Stein, Susie Johnson

Tami Cowles, Terri Adkisson

Wendy Schindler

PATREON SUPPORTERS

Exclusive short stories
Premium Access to works in progress
Free Ebooks for select tiers

Join here
The Magick Squad

THANK YOU

Aaron Matthews, Alisha Harper, Amber Dawn Sessler, Angela Tapping, Anne Morando, Anthony Hudson, Ashley Britt

Brenda French, Brent Lowe

Carolyn J. Evans, Carrie O'Leary, Christopher Scoggins, Cindy Deporter, Connie Cleary, Cooper Walls

Dan Bergemann, Dan Fong, David Smith, Davis Johnson, Diane Garcia, Diane Jackson, Diane Kassmann, Dorothy Phillips

Elizabeth Varga, Enid Rodriguez, Eric Maldonado, Eve Bartlet, Ewan Mollison

Federica De Dominicis, Fluff Chick Productions, Gail Ketcham Hermann, Gary McVicar, Groove72

Heidi Wolfe

Ingrid Schijven

James Burns, James Wheat, Jasmine Breeden, Jasmine Davis, Jeffrey Juchau, Jo Dungey, Joe Durham, John Fauver(*in memoriam*), Joy Kiili, Just Jeanette

Krista Fox

Leona Jackson, Lisa Simpson, Lizzette Piltch

Malcolm Robertson, Mark Morgan, Mark Price, Mary Beth Wright, MaryAnn Sims, Maureen McCallan, Mel Brown, Melissa Miller, Meri, Duncanson

Paige Guido, Patricia Pearson, Peter Griffin, Pete Peters

Ralph Kroll, Renee Penn, Rick Clapp, Robert Walters

Sara M Branson, Sara N Morgan, Sarah Sofianos, Sassy Bear, Sharon Elliott, Shelby, Sonyia Roy, Stacey Stein, Steven Huber, Susan Bowin, Susan Spry

Tami Cowles, Terri Adkisson, Tommy, Trish Brown

Van Nebedum

W S Dawkins, Wendy Schindler, Wicketbird

***

I want to extend a special note of gratitude to all of our Patrons in
The Magick Squad.

Your generous support helps me to continue on this amazing adventure called 'being an author'.
I deeply and truly appreciate each of you for your selfless act of patronage.

You are all amazing beyond belief.

THANK YOU

ACKNOWLEDGEMENTS

With each book, I realize that every time I learn something about this craft, it highlights so many things I still have to learn. Each book, each creative expression, has a large group of people behind it.

This book is no different.

Even though you see one name on the cover, it is with the knowledge that I am standing on the shoulders of the literary giants that informed my youth, and am supported by my generous readers who give of their time to jump into the adventures of my overactive imagination.

I would like to take a moment to express my most sincere thanks:

To Dolly: My wife and greatest support. You make all this possible each and every day. You keep me grounded when I get lost in the forest of ideas. Thank you for asking the right questions when needed, and listening intently when I go off on tangents. Thank you for who you are and the space you create—I love you.

To my Tribe: You are the reason I have stories to tell. You cannot possibly fathom how much and how deeply I love you all.

To Lee: Because you were the first audience I ever had. I love you, sis.

To the Logsdon Family: The words *thank you* are insufficient to describe the gratitude in my heart for each of you. JL, your support always demands I bring my best, my A-game, and produce the best story I can. Both you and Lorelei (my Uber Jeditor) and now, Audrey, are the reason I am where I am today. My thank you for the notes, challenges, corrections, advice, and laughter. Your patience is truly infinite. *Arigatogozaimasu.*

To The Montague & Strong Case Files Group—AKA The MoB (Mages of Badassery): When I wrote T&B there were fifty-five members in The MoB. As of this release, there are over one thousand five hundred members in the MoB. I am honored to be able to call you my MoB Family. Thank you for being part of this group and M&S.

You make this possible. **THANK YOU.**

To the ever-vigilant PACK: You help make the MoB...the MoB. Keeping it a safe place for us to share and just...be. Thank you for your selfless vigilance. You truly are the Sentries of Sanity.

Chris Christman II: A real-life technomancer who makes the **MoBTV LIVEvents +Kaffeeklatsch** on YouTube amazing. Thank you for your tireless work and wisdom. Everything is connected...you totally rock!

To the WTA—The Incorrigibles: JL, Ben Z., Eric QK., S.S., and Noah.

They sound like a bunch of badass misfits, because they are. My exposure to the deranged and deviant brain trust you all represent helped me be the author I am today. I have officially gone to the *dark side* thanks to all of you. I humbly give you my thanks, and...it's all your fault.

To my fellow Indie Authors: I want to thank each of you for creating a space where authors can feel listened to, and encouraged to continue on this path. A rising tide lifts all the ships indeed.

To The English Advisory: Aaron, Penny, Carrie, Davina, and all of the UK MoB. For all things English...thank you.

To DEATH WISH COFFEE: This book (and every book I write) has been fueled by generous amounts of the only coffee on the planet (and in space) strong enough to power my very twisted imagination. Is there any other coffee that can compare? I think not. DEATH WISH—thank you!

To Deranged Doctor Design: Kim, Darja, Tanja, Jovana, and Milo (Designer Extraordinaire).

If you've seen the covers of my books and been amazed, you can thank the very talented and gifted creative team at DDD. They take the rough ideas I give them, and produce incredible covers that continue to surprise and amaze me. Each time, I find myself striving to write a story worthy of the covers they produce. DDD, you embody professionalism and creativity. Thank you for the great service and spectacular covers. **YOU GUYS RULE!**

To you, the reader: I was always taught to save the best for last. I write these stories for **you**. Thank you for jumping down the rabbit holes of ***what if?*** with me. You are the reason I write the stories I do.

You keep reading...I'll keep writing.

Thank you for your support and encouragement.

SPECIAL MENTIONS

To Dolly: my rock, anchor, and inspiration. Thank you...always.

Larry & Tammy—The WOUF: Because even when you aren't there...you're there.

Orlando A. Sanchez
www.orlandoasanchez.com

Orlando has been writing ever since his teens when he was immersed in creating scenarios for playing Dungeons and Dragons with his friends every weekend.

The worlds of his books are urban settings with a twist of the paranormal lurking just behind the scenes and with generous doses of magic, martial arts, and mayhem.

He currently resides in Queens, NY with his wife and children.

Thanks for Reading!

If you enjoyed this book
Please leave a review & share!
(with everyone you know)

It would really help us out!

Printed in Great Britain
by Amazon